S0-AWF-260

JAKE

THIS BOOK IS A GIFT
OF FRIENDS
OF THE ORINDA LIBRARY

ALSO BY AUDREY COULOUMBIS

Getting Near to Baby

Love Me Tender

Maude March on the Run!

The Misadventures of Maude March

Say Yes

Summer's End

War Games (with Akila Couloumbis)

JAKE

WITHDRAWN

Audrey Couloumbis

Random House 🏠 New York

This is a work of fiction. Names, characters, places, and incidents either are the product of the author's imagination or are used fictitiously. Any resemblance to actual persons, living or dead, events, or locales is entirely coincidental.

Text copyright © 2010 by Audrey Couloumbis
Jacket art copyright © 2010 by Antonio Javier Caparo

All rights reserved.

Published in the United States by Random House Children's Books, a division of Random House, Inc., New York.

Random House and the colophon are registered trademarks of Random House, Inc.

Visit us on the Web! www.randomhouse.com/kids

Educators and librarians, for a variety of teaching tools, visit us at www.randomhouse.com/teachers

Library of Congress Cataloging-in-Publication Data
Couloumbis, Audrey.
Jake / by Audrey Couloumbis. — 1st ed.
p. cm.
Summary: When ten-year-old Jake's widowed mother breaks her leg just before Christmas while her sister and best friend are both away, a grandfather Jake barely remembers must come to Baltimore, Maryland, to help a neighbor take care of him.
ISBN 978-0-375-85630-3 (trade) — ISBN 978-0-375-95630-0 (lib. bdg.) — ISBN 978-0-375-89321-6 (e-book) — ISBN 978-0-375-85631-0 (pbk.)
[1. Grandfathers—Fiction. 2. Neighbors—Fiction. 3. Hospitals—Fiction. 4. Accidents—Fiction. 5. Single-parent families—Fiction. 6. Christmas—Fiction. 7. Baltimore (Md.)—Fiction.] I. Title.
PZ7.C8305Jak 2010
[Fic]—dc22
2009029383

Printed in the United States of America
10 9 8 7 6 5 4 3 2 1

First Edition

Random House Children's Books supports the First Amendment and celebrates the right to read.

*To a mysterious bald person
who prefers to go unnamed*

"Joey Ziglar says it's boring, grocery shopping with his mom," I said. It was our usual Saturday-afternoon trip to the store.

"Lucky for you, I'm not Joey Ziglar's mom."

"It's a little boring," I said. "Sometimes."

"You've got your own list and a budget," Mom said. "What more do you want? A dance routine?"

"We-ell—"

"Get real," she said with a little smile.

"A lot of the stuff on my list is a snore," I said. "Bread, cereal, canned tuna. Juice boxes, milk, and ice cream."

"You weren't listening," she said. "You have a budget. Figure out how to get yourself a treat out of it."

It took me nearly an hour to do it. I mean, there's just one canned tuna we like. And we always try to pick ice cream that's on sale. Where's the wiggle room?

I found it. Two boxes of cereal cost an amazing amount of money—more than ice cream. Oatmeal is cheap and healthy. Cocoa Puffs are neither. Cocoa Puffs don't taste as good as big, soft cookies that could be homemade, so that decision practically made itself. Mom spotted the oatmeal in my cart. "Figured out how to buy treats on your budget?"

"Cookies," I said. "Big, soft cookies."

Mom's eyes lit up. "What kind?"

"White chocolate with some kind of nuts. And chocolate chip."

"Good picks." She looked pretty cheerful about the cookies. She likes the ones with the strange nuts.

I pushed the filled-to-the-top grocery cart outside. Everything up to this point was like any other Saturday.

As we walked out to the car—no, as we skidded and skated across the icy parking lot, sometimes sliding away and then coming back together like we each held the end of a rubber band—Mom said, "Let's make one more trip to the mall. Last-minute Christmas shopping."

My hopes that she'd be looking for a bicycle sank. If I was going with her, she wasn't shopping for me.

I would stand in line to hold the space, and then I'd carry the bag. I shoved the grocery cart around our car to the passenger side, huffing it over an icy ridge running along the ground. "I'm old enough to stay home alone, I hope you know."

Mom said, "Not a chance. Who's going to lug the loot ba—" and the locks on the car doors sprang open. I opened the door and unloaded the cart, putting everything on the floor in front of the backseat. It took five minutes, probably less.

"Mom?" I said, looking around when I'd finished. I didn't see her.

"Mom!" I yelled. "Mom?"

CHAPTER ONE

This Saturday had started out like any old weekend. We slept later than on a school morning, just not as late as on Sunday morning.

I was up earlier than usual this Saturday. I had a mission.

I sneaked into Mom's darkened room. She was snoring a little. I waited a second to see if she'd wake up and then I tiptoed to her closet. It was the likeliest hiding place now that I'd ruled out Aunt Ginny's and our friend Suzie's closets.

The jumble of Mom's shoes across the floor seemed undisturbed. The clothes, on the other hand, never looked the same to me, as if shirts and pants on a hanger and a few dresses changed places when no one was home. I reached in, running my arm through the dark space at each end of the closet, hoping to find a bike standing on the back tire. When I leaned in a little, I felt the wall. No bike. No luck.

Behind me, Mom sighed a little. I shut the closet door partway, like I'd found it.

"Mom, it's nine-thirty."

She pulled the covers over her head.

"Rise and shine," I said, heading for her windows.

"I'm shining," Mom said. "Can't the rising wait another five minutes?"

"Only if you're a loaf of bread. Think of Master Kim telling us, 'Twenty-five push-ups for tardy.'"

I yanked on a roller shade and let it go. It racketed to the top of the window and snapped to a halt. The blast of sunshine hurt my eyes for a second, even though I'd already been up for ten minutes.

"Aaaaah," my mom yelled. "Death rays!"

Sunshine reflecting off snow and ice is like sunlight supercharged. If you close your eyes after you look, the inside of your eyelids are white, white, white.

"I'm feeding the fish." I went away, knowing Mom wouldn't get up yet. She never got up on the first call. This used to bother me a lot more when I was younger, like seven or eight. It was almost scary sometimes.

For one thing, I had to catch a bus.

If you saw the look that driver gave me after she

had to wait a few seconds for me to leave Mom and run the last half block, you'd be scared too.

But ten is a turning point, maturity-wise, Aunt Ginny says.

I can really feel it. It doesn't bother me so much that Mom isn't always the one in charge. Plus, it makes me feel more grown-up when I'm in charge.

Sometimes, just sometimes, I wish we were more than the two of us. Then if Mom was having one of her not-in-charge moments, somebody else could pick up the slack.

Not that I want somebody to think it's their job to boss me around. Just a person who knew it was their turn to take over sometimes.

I stood in Mom's doorway.

"Toaster waffles after we eat an egg," I said, the way Mom did when she was the first one up. It was the same breakfast every Saturday.

"Okay, okay, I'm getting up."

So I got out of there. Mom sleeps in her underpants and a T-shirt.

I never noticed this until Matthew Haygood said in class that's what his mom slept in. Our health teacher, Mrs. Baggs, sent the social worker around to his house.

His mom hadn't been told anybody was coming. She answered the door in the same outfit. What happened after that, Matthew had to go spend three weeks with his grandmother, who lived two blocks away.

His mom had to go to court to say she was physically fit or had a fit, or something fit, anyway. Which maybe wouldn't have been enough to convince the judge, except Matthew's grandmother went to court that day with her lawyer.

Matthew said his grandmother told them *she* didn't sleep in anything at all and they thought Matthew was safe enough with *her*, so who were they kidding?

Matthew loves that part; he even took me into the kitchen and begged his grandmother to say it again the way she said it that day, and she did. She said it exactly.

It wasn't so much *what* she said as the way she said it. Like she thought they could all be replaced by hockey pucks and no one would notice. If I ever went to court, I'd want Matthew's grandmother on my side.

His grandmother told me the lawyer said legal things. He also said Matthew's mom answered the door that way because her mother lived two blocks away and visited every day. She expected it would be her mother at the door.

The upshot of it was, Matthew got to go home.

But it looked bad there for a while.

Single mothers have to be really careful is what Mom said when she heard about this. I had never heard Mom call herself a single mother. Or maybe it was the first time anything made me think about it.

Maybe I'd only ever noticed when she told people she's a widow. Until Matthew and his mom had that trouble, being a widow sounded so much worse than being a single mother.

I don't remember having a dad. Well. Certain things. A deep voice. A certain way of being carried under someone's arm so my arms and legs hung like a dog's. Someone who could bounce on my bed so hard I'd lift off the mattress, and all the time I was laughing like a maniac. I wish I remembered my dad better.

The trouble with memory is you can't tell the difference between what's real and what you accidentally made up. One time, Mom asked me, "What do you remember about your dad?"

We were sitting elbow to elbow on the couch so we could share the popcorn. She'd turned down the sound on the commercials. So I told her all these things about the voice and bouncing on the bed.

I also thought of this one memory that I sometimes

get when we're near people smoking a cigarette. First, it's the smell of the smoke. Then I'm sitting on somebody's lap and there's a low voice in my ear, singing—I know this sounds weird—that counting song about beer bottles on the wall. The first time I heard that song when it wasn't in memory, the hair stood up on my arms.

I told Mom how important that smell felt to me. How I started to pay attention to smokers until I figured out only Camel cigarettes mattered. She gave me a strange look and said, "Your dad didn't smoke."

The commercials weren't over but she turned the sound up.

We don't talk about what I remember about my dad anymore. I still like the smell of Camel cigarettes, even knowing it isn't a Dad memory. I breathe deep whenever we pass someone with that smell floating around them.

Even knowing cigarette smoke is bad.

It probably doesn't matter whether my memories are perfect. Cigarette smoke made me feel like I remember my dad. That was better than nothing.

So this Saturday, we left the breakfast dishes in the sink. Mom said we needed the extra five minutes to dress warmly. We put on long underwear and knotted scarves around our necks like snowmen. We still got cold standing in the elevator.

"It's going to be brutal outside," Mom said, like she was thinking about turning around and going back to bed.

"Joey Ziglar's dad says the elevator shaft works like a thermometer. The cold comes from the basement, where there isn't much heat because heat rises. The cold follows it up the shaft like mercury."

"Thanks for that bulletin," Mom said, rolling her eyes.

The lobby, usually shadowy, was bright with reflected sunlight. The plants around the fountain looked more enthusiastic than at any other time of year. Or maybe the super, Mr. G, made it look that way by adding all these red flowers in pots for the holidays.

We zipped through the doors in our usual hurry and stopped. The first couple of seconds outside took our breath away.

Mom and I looked at each other with scream faces, then ducked back into the lobby for a second to let ourselves get used to it. "Cold out there," I said, sort of gasping.

Mom kept jumping from foot to foot, warm-ups.

My eyes teared up when the wind hit me. It's cool

really. Everything looks like it has such sharp edges for a few minutes after that happens.

"I'm gonna beat your butt in class," Mom said.

Okay, so there was no turning back. We charged outside again.

The wind blew so hard my scarf stood straight out over my shoulder. A fresh layer of snow had fallen overnight, and the wind picked it up, so that it danced through the air like crisp, cold bees, stinging our faces.

We turned the corner of the building to get to the car, and walking in the shade there, the wind wasn't so bad. We were too cold to talk, though. Mom says the air makes the fillings in her teeth hurt.

Then we got out in the sun again. It was better in the sun. Not really warm, but better.

We scraped an eggshell-thin layer of ice off the windows and mirrors while the car warmed up. I like doing this. The ice falls away in dinner plate–sized sheets that make a sound like *crickle-crackle*. It looks like broken glass when it hits the ground.

I said, "What did you get me for Christmas, that's what I want to know."

"For me to know, for you to wonder and worry," Mom said, not wanting to open her mouth too much.

We go to karate class first.

My mom and I take class together. It's sort of hard to live down, taking class with Mom. She says, if one of us has to quit, I'm going to get awful cold waiting in the car for her because *she's* not embarrassed to be seen in class with me.

Or without me.

So neither one of us is going to quit.

Next is grocery shopping.

Everything up to this point was like any other Saturday. Well, except for the hundred Christmas trees lined up in front of the store for people to choose from.

Lately it smells like walking through a pine forest to go buy bread. A Santa Claus rang a bell for people to drop money in his Meaty Bone box for the dog pound. Even dogs get Christmas, I guess.

More pine forest as we left. I kept trying to get Christmas present hints out of Mom. As we skidded and skated across the icy parking lot, she planned the rest of our day.

Shopping, shopping, and shopping.

When we got to our car, I had to work the grocery cart over an icy ridge. I didn't need any help. Karate has made me strong. I said, "I'm old enough to stay home alone, I hope you know."

Mom said, "Not a chance. Who's going to lug the loot ba—" and the locks on the car doors sprang open. I lost the rest of what she said as the cart rattled over that last icy bump.

I unloaded the cart, putting everything on the floor in front of the backseat. It took five minutes, probably less.

"Mom?" I said, looking around when I'd finished. I didn't see her.

"Mom!" I yelled. "Mom?"

This old lady who was slipping and sliding along behind her cart looked my way. I yelled, "Mom," then she yelled and pointed at the car. At the other side of the car, so I ran—slid—around there.

Mom had fallen on the ice.

She'd slipped partway under the car. She was white, almost like the ice, her face pinched in a way I had never seen. It was a lot more slippery on this side of the car. The ice was wetter, like somebody had spilled something there. I fell on my butt getting to Mom.

I hardly felt myself hit. For a second, everything went black.

I'd heard someone say that once in a movie. I pictured it like Suzie's darkroom where she makes her camera film into photographs. You switch off the light and you have this little bit of light in your memory so you have a second or two to get used to the black.

It wasn't like that. I was in the dark so fast I didn't know it until the light was coming back.

I felt numb as I got up; I couldn't move as fast as I wanted to. Something did hurt. I couldn't tell what, and I didn't feel like thinking about it.

Mom hadn't moved. That old lady never stopped yelling. I liked that. By the time I got on my knees next to my mom, help was arriving. The Santa. Then four or five more people.

"Mom," I said. I put my hand on hers, not sure where she hurt, or if I could make it worse. She grabbed me and held on tight. She hadn't said anything. I looked up, saying, "She's hurt."

"Somebody call an ambulance," a man in a store jacket said over the other voices.

"Mom," I said again. I couldn't get over it. I ran the idea through my mind a few times. Not like a thought, over and over, but something I had to figure out.

Mom worries about something like this happening to me. Not out loud. But when she hesitates a little before she says yes to rock climbing with Aunt

Ginny and then adds, "Be careful," I get it that she's worried. When she won't buy me a bike, I get it.

And now I could see her point. I was right here when this happened and I didn't even know it for whole minutes. And there was nothing I could do to help.

Another few people came to look, including a woman with a crying baby on her hip. The baby kept crying and crying. The mom paid no attention to it at all. When the ambulance came screaming down the street, it took me a minute to know the difference.

The old lady, the first to notice Mom had fallen, said very loudly, "I feel better knowing help has arrived and I'm going now." She turned to the woman with the crying baby and said, even more loudly, "I'd advise you to do the same, so the medics can hear themselves think."

For a moment there, I just loved that old lady.

CHAPTER TWO

It was a broken leg, that's what the medic guys said. They made me ride up front in the ambulance, like a copilot. The real copilot rode in the back with Mom, sitting where I would rather have been.

I think I would.

Mom had begun to moan a lot and that made me feel sick, even from up front. The pilot—the driver, that is—tried to take my mind off Mom.

He asked, "What's your favorite sport?"

I couldn't think of any sports. I stared at him. He was wearing this knit cap with a pom-pom dangling down his neck. I'd get beaten up in the school yard wearing a hat like that.

He ran the siren through a busy part of town. Green ropes of tinsel and little Christmas flags were strung between the streetlights. Cars pulled over to the side of the road so we could rush past them.

While all this noise was filling our heads, the driver looked over and grinned like a crazy person in a scary movie I saw once at Matthew's house. He even had the same pointy eyebrows.

He definitely didn't look like somebody Mom would let drive us anywhere. I almost wished *he* were the one riding in the back. Except Mom had enough problems without him sitting next to her.

When he stopped at the hospital, he said, "Great ride, huh?"

I knew he'd been trying to make me feel better. It didn't work, that's all. I climbed out and hurried around the ambulance.

There was no ice in this parking area, so it was easy for them to lift Mom out of there and push her inside on this bed with wheels. A gurney, they called it.

More noise came at me in the hospital. Squeaky wheels. A doctor yelling questions at us. The ambulance guys yelling back. Somebody crying. Was that Mom crying?

People moved fast. I ran behind the gurney till somebody pulled a curtain closed right in front of my face. The ambulance driver said, "She's gotta do this by herself."

I didn't like the sound of that.

He walked me to a desk where he said, "I've gotta move the truck."

He put some woman in charge of me. She barked questions at me like a seal. "Can you call your dad? Where do you live? How old is your mother? What's her insurance company? Who's her doctor? Which relative do you call in an emergency?"

"I don't know," I said. That felt wrong. I was sure I knew the name of the doctor Mom went to. Probably I knew everywhere she sent checks because she usually talked to herself while she wrote them. No names came to mind. My mind went blue, like a computer waiting for someone to choose a screen saver.

The other guy from the ambulance came and said, "You should follow the gurney upstairs."

He put me on an elevator. "Get off on ten," he said, and pushed ten like I was too young to know.

Other people got on and off at the third floor, and the fourth, and the seventh and ninth. Because they were patients, none of them looked like anybody I usually saw on elevators. I tried not to stare at the ones with plastic tubes taped to their arms or sitting in wheelchairs.

In the end, I was glad he told me to get off on ten and pushed the button to be sure I would.

At the desk, I said, "Can I see my mom? She just got here."

A nurse said, "Sit over there."

There was Christmas music playing. It sounded sort of too slow, like the tape player needed batteries.

I could have looked out the windows, I guess. I sat there, thinking my butt still hurt, like that should matter, and bit all my fingernails down. Mom hates nail biting. I figured she wouldn't care much that I was doing it right now.

After a while, another woman came to talk to me. Not a nurse; she wore a skirt and sweater like she worked in an office. She said I should call her Miss Sahara, like the desert. I think this was supposed to be funny, only I couldn't smile. Besides, she was smiling hard enough for both of us.

Miss Sahara told me the insurance stuff could wait, but she needed to know what relative to call. Did my mom have any allergies or illnesses they ought to know about? "Can't Mom answer any of this?"

"The doctor gave her a sedative."

"What does that mean?"

"They put her to sleep."

"To sleep?" I stood straight out of my chair.

Mom had our cat put to sleep last year because she was old and sick. Mom wasn't either one of those things. Tears started running down my face. I must've looked like a big baby but I didn't care.

"I didn't even get to talk to her."

The weird thing is, somebody tells you your mom is dead, you'd think it would be like stuff they say on television, your heart would be breaking.

Only my heart was sort of numb. My voice went away entirely and it was my jaw that might break. My mouth was wide open. I wasn't making a sound and I couldn't close it.

I never cried like that before.

Miss Sahara kept on smiling and listing diseases I mostly never heard of. This guy in a white coat—maybe he was a doctor only not in a big hurry to go anywhere—came over and said, "What's going on here?"

She showed him even more teeth and said, "I'm trying to sort things out. We're having a little melt-down here."

"I thought," I managed to say, "it was just a broken leg."

My voice came out so hoarse, I don't think they understood me. She looked away and talked to him in a lower voice, as if I had left the room. "His mother's the spiral fracture. No purse, and she's out like a light."

"Okay, fella, deep breath. Way deep," the guy said. I noticed his name tag, it said STAN. Stan the man, I'd heard that somewhere. "Everything's going to be fine. Just you and your mom out together today?"

I tried to get a deep breath that wasn't the kind that had to do with crying. I had this feeling like a belt pulled tight around my chest.

"Shake your head yes or no."

I shook yes.

"Your dad at home?"

No.

"Your dad live with you?"

No.

"Got a grandma or grandpa?"

Yes. A grandfather.

I never saw him. I talked to him on the phone at Christmas and my birthday, that was about it.

While I was answering Stan, my jaw started to relax. He saw that, I guess, because he sat down and waited for me to be able to talk. "It was a broken leg," I said, finally.

Miss Sahara's smile shrank just enough to look like I'd said something stupid. "A spiral fracture is—"

"—a certain kind of broken leg," Stan said.

"That can be fixed," I said. "They didn't have to put her to sleep."

Now it was Stan who looked like somebody'd said something stupid. Only he looked that look at Miss Sahara, who turned red.

"Your mom's going to be okay," he said to me. "The doctor gave her something to *help* her sleep so she wouldn't be in pain."

"She's not dead?"

"No way, man," Stan said. "Sleeping like a baby. They're going to have to operate, though. Miss Sahara, here, it's her job to ask you questions your mom can't answer now."

The tears didn't quit. They ran so fast I couldn't keep my eyes open. My face sort of crumpled. My breath came faster.

"Hang on, hang on," Stan said. "Your mom's fine. At least, she's going to be."

It took a minute but I started to feel like I knew

that. The tears stopped. I could breathe the way I usually did. Stan looked at me like I was somebody he already knew, which sounds strange but felt good.

I looked at Miss Sahara. She still had that awful smile on her face.

"So," she said, making it sound the way a bird chirps. "Does your mother take medication for anything?"

"Aspirin, sometimes."

"Anything give her a rash?"

"Mangos make her look like a blowfish."

"Mangos," she said as if it was good news. She wrote it down. "Anything else?"

I shook my head no.

"No worries there, then," she said, getting ready to write. "Let's get to you. Your name?"

"Jake Wexler."

"Jake. What's that short for?"

"It's Jake on my birth certificate," I said, as I sometimes have to do. We went through a list; I sat down carefully, because I had fallen on my butt. I told her Mom's name and our address and other stuff. I remembered who Mom's doctor is.

"Now about somebody to call," Miss Sahara said.

"For what?"

"To take care of you," she said in a let's-go-to-a-party voice. She was starting to get on my nerves. "Any family living nearby?"

I shook my head again.

Stan asked, "Where do your grandma and grandpa live?"

"North Carolina. Granddad." Mom calls him Granddad when she's talking to me, anyway. "The others have all died."

You'd think it would be good to have the one. I mean, I'd like to have grandparents like anybody else. I could be happy with only the one, but we don't visit my dad's dad and it's weird talking to somebody you only know by their voice and a few old pictures. I never got around to calling him anything. I'd say hi, we'd go through a couple of the usual *How's school?* kind of questions, we'd say good-bye politely, and that was it.

"Well, that's not too far away." Stan said. "Grand-dad. Where in North Carolina?"

"My mom wouldn't call him. So I don't think you should either."

Stan said, "Maybe there's a friend of your mom's you could stay with?"

Miss Sahara said, "We need the name of another blood relative."

"There's Aunt Ginny," I said. "She's away."

"Away?" This was Miss Sahara and she sounded like somehow Aunt Ginny should have known better than to go away this weekend. "Perhaps we should tell her she's needed here?"

"We can't," I said. "She takes women out for wilderness weekends, and nobody uses a phone. That includes her."

"Cool," Stan said and then frowned. "Cold."

"They're in a desert in Arizona this time."

Stan grinned. "Very cool."

"Surely they do have an emergency phone," Miss Sahara said.

"Nope," I said. "Well, if somebody gets hurt, Aunt Ginny can call for help, but we can't phone her, It's against the rules and she keeps her phone turned off. She gets back on Tuesday, though."

"Any close friends?"

"Suzie. Can't get her either."

"Where might *she* be?"

"She's on a Greenpeace boat in the Pacific Ocean."

"Really very cool," Stan said.

Miss Sahara said, "Any friends from your mother's workplace?"

"Mom works at home."

"What does *she* do?" This was Stan.

"She translates books to English," I said. "Mostly about how people act. Behavioral science, that's it."

"Wow, what languages?"

"German, Danish, and Swedish."

Stan sat back a little. Something about this impresses people. "It's cool," I said.

"It's the coolest of all," he said.

I nodded, glad that Stan got it that Mom did something as interesting as Aunt Ginny or Suzie.

Even I didn't get it until this time I caught Mom doing a happy dance of having found just the right words. She was quiet, and there was no music, but the happy dance said it all.

So did the ice-cream sundaes we made right after. Just thinking about it almost made me cry again. I missed Mom, but mostly I missed the way we felt that day.

I gave Miss Sahara Granddad's name. Ned Wexler. He was my dad's dad and Mom is always careful that he knows she's doing a good job with me. She can't be blamed for breaking her leg, but then, Granddad always sounded a little stiff.

That was all I knew about him. I started to wish I had a real grandparent, like Matthew's grandma. I mean, Granddad sent presents at birthdays and Christmas. I had a present from him under the tree. It was always whatever Mom told him I wanted—without her help, he wouldn't know what I'd like.

I didn't know what he'd like either. Mom always sent him cigars.

I wished I could stay with Matthew Haygood's grandmother.

"What about your school friends?" Miss Sahara said. "For one night."

There was Joey Ziglar. Mrs. Ziglar liked me. But Joey's family had already started for Florida, to see more family during the holidays.

I thought about asking Mrs. Baxter if I could sleep over. The last time I did, Jerry broke a window and I said I did it so he wouldn't get grounded from hockey practice. I don't think his mom would want me much.

Matthew Haygood's mom and mine weren't friendly enough for sleepovers. Mom still sort of sided with her on the T-shirt and panties thing, though.

Mom liked Sarah Jane's mom, but I didn't want to spend the night on Sarah Jane's couch. If Sarah Jane woke up before I did and saw me sleeping with my mouth open or something, it would be all over school in no time.

I shook my head.

"We need a name to call for overnight."

I stared at her.

"You can't stay here all night," she said. "You have to sleep somewhere."

Looking out the window then, I saw it was practically dark outside. I missed lunch and didn't even notice. It didn't seem like we'd been away from home all that long. Of course, it got dark early in winter.

"You can come back tomorrow, of course. So who are we calling?"

"Mrs. Buttermark, I guess. Our neighbor. She's sort of old, but we hang out together sometimes."

"Hang out?"

"That's what we say we're doing," I said. "She doesn't think I need a babysitter either."

"She ought to do." She looked like Mrs. Buttermark got an A+.

Here I was wracking my brain for the actual people Mom would let me stay with. I could give her anybody's name and she would be saying, "She ought to do."

I decided not to point this out to Miss Sahara. Really, how much more time did I want to spend with *her*?

"Mrs. Buttermark. Her number?" Miss Sahara's smile didn't keep her from sounding like that thin ice that Mom and I scraped off the windshield. *Crickle-crackle.*

Miss Sahara wrote the number down, then said, "Have you ever spent the night with her before?"

"She stayed with us a few times. Last month when her bathroom was being fixed, and once when Mom had a bad cold. Then again when *she* caught the flu."

Miss Sahara looked happy to hear it. "Definitely our best choice."

"I should talk to her first," I said. "So she doesn't get too worried."

"Good idea," Miss Sahara said.

"Also, can I tell her you'll put me in a taxi? That way she doesn't have to worry about cleaning off her windshield and stuff."

"That's not the way we do things," Miss Sahara said.

"Mrs. Buttermark is a lot older than my mom."

This was true, even if I did forget it sometimes. "If she breaks *her* leg getting here, there's no one else."

"I live over that way," Stan said. "If he sits ten more minutes, my shift is over and I can drive him home."

Miss Sahara said, "Stanley—"

"Stan. That's how it reads on my birth certificate."

Her smile wobbled. "Stan. It's against the rules."

"Blink," Stan said. "You won't see a thing."

"Well," Miss Sahara said, making the word into a sigh. "Let's start with your grandfather anyway. What's his phone number?"

I didn't know. It was like she hadn't listened to me at all. I said, "Let's call Mrs. Buttermark."

"*Sit* here," Miss Sahara said, standing up. "Don't go wandering around."

Stan said, "He'd be better off over in the next wing. There's a TV in the waiting room there. Take his mind off things."

"Oh, all right," Miss Sahara said.

CHAPTER THREE

"You hungry?" Stan asked me as we walked away from the bad tape of Christmas music.

"Not really." I was tired. Miss Sahara sort of wore me out with all that smiling. It would be rude to say so. Also, it worried me that she was going to call my granddad. I didn't think Mom would like that.

She doesn't talk much with my granddad. More than I did, but not like she'd talk to one of her friends. I didn't know what to do about Miss Sahara or anything she was planning.

"So your mom fell on the ice, huh?"

"Yeah."

"Do you think your mom's purse got left where she fell or something?" Stan said. "Because nobody brought it in. I'm thinking her credit cards and stuff might be lost."

"Mom doesn't carry a purse since it got grabbed away from her once. There's a waterproof pocket in the jacket she was wearing. All her money and her driver's license and stuff goes into that pocket."

"I think they looked in her coat."

"It's hidden under the pocket flap where there's a regular pocket too," I said. "The coat's special. The same kind Aunt Ginny takes into the wilderness when she's going somewhere cold."

So we went to get Mom's coat.

On the way, I asked him, "How long till Mom's better?"

"A couple of months," Stan said. "She'll get out of the cast and then do some exercise to make sure she builds up muscle again."

I waited outside the room Stan went into. He brought Mom's coat out, and I went through the pocket to find her insurance card. Stan had somebody at the desk make a copy and then he gave it to me.

"You ought to take the jacket home with you for now," he said. "Your mom won't need it here. When they give her a locker, you can bring whatever stuff she asks for."

"Can I call Mrs. Buttermark now?"

"Let's do it."

He asked the nurse at the desk to let us use her phone. She dialed a couple of numbers, listened, and handed me the receiver. It had a regular dial tone coming out of it.

"Dial your number," the nurse said.

Mrs. Buttermark answered. She lives alone.

"It's Jake," I said. "Mom broke her leg and has to stay at the hospital. Can I sleep over?"

"Of course you can," she said. "Which hospital are you at? I'll come get you."

"I have a ride," I said. "We aren't leaving this minute. I don't know what time I'll get there."

"Don't worry about that. I'll be up."

Stan sat down with me in the waiting room. He picked up the remote and flipped channels. While we stared at the TV, my brain started to work again.

When I had my tonsils out, Mom slept in a chair next to my hospital bed. If they sent me home, there was no one to be with her. That bothered me.

After Mom got through the operation, what then? How long would she be in the hospital? How long did we need to have someone to help?

Did we have to move in with Aunt Ginny? Or

would she move in with us? I could live with one short-haired cat if we turned on the air conditioner once a day. But my allergy pills were no match for Aunt Ginny's three long-haired cats. What would we do about that?

It wasn't the most important question at that moment, but I wondered what we'd do about Christmas, if it would come and go while Mom was in the hospital.

While the list of things to worry about got longer, Miss Sahara came back. I said, "Are they operating on my mom yet?"

"No, no," she said as if she were tamping down a fire. "Not till Monday anyway. A doctor has to take her case."

"I want to see her."

She said, "That's not a good idea."

"I think you can," Stan said. "She's sleeping and she isn't going to wake up even for you. The medicine does that. You understand?"

"I'm ten, not three."

"Look, it's hard for grown-ups to get the message sometimes," he said. "I don't want it to scare you that she won't wake up."

"It won't scare me."

It did, though.

This was not how Mom looked when she was sleeping. She was flat on her back with her leg packed in ice, and her face looked wrong somehow. Too still.

She looked more like a mask of herself.

When I touched her hand, she didn't grab for mine. She didn't know I was there. Like *really* didn't know I was there. I'd never gotten that feeling before.

I felt like crying again.

Even in the morning it was more like she was *trying* to sleep soundly when I went into her room. It was like some small part of her sleeping brain already knew I was on my way. I could sneak in, but I pretty much knew if she'd had a bike in the closet, she'd have been wide awake fast.

"She's okay," Stan said.

At least she's warm, I thought. That means she isn't dead. "Well, then," I said. "I'm ready to go."

"You sure?"

I sort of wanted to get out of there. "Mrs. Buttermark is waiting for me. She might start to worry."

I know I wanted to see her, and I was glad I did. But it felt worse to be standing next to her and not be able to tell her how scary this all was. It wasn't that I was afraid I'd cry again. I was afraid I'd hold on to her wrist and not let go, like I did when I was a really little kid and didn't want to go to nursery school.

On the drive, Stan talked about how cool Mom and Aunt Ginny and Suzie must be. He kept asking questions. Not nosy ones. More the admiring kind.

I told him how Suzie doesn't say men and women, she says male and female. Everything is science with her. And Aunt Ginny is a daredevil, that's what Mom calls her. I said, "If Aunt Ginny was my mom, I'd have a bicycle by now."

"Your mom got something against bikes?"

"My dad got hit by a truck while he was riding one. It's made her kinda nervous about them."

"That's gotta be hard on her. You can see that."

I wanted a bike. I couldn't be mad about not getting one, that was the hard part. I shifted in the car seat to get off the achy part of my butt.

I was holding Mom's coat, and it smelled like her. Part curry powder that she likes to cook with and part sweet orange that her face cream smells like and part this dry silver plant with round leaves that she puts all around the apartment. I got real tired in the car. I think I fell asleep for a minute.

Mrs. Buttermark met Stan and me at the door in

her dressed-up-to-go-out look. This always reminds me that she's old, the way she dresses up to meet people.

"Would you like to come in?" she asked him. "I make a mean hot chocolate."

"No, thank you," Stan said.

Mrs. Buttermark is no pushover, that's what Mom says about her. In about three minutes she had him in her kitchen, making a fuss over him being the kind of young man people look up to. "Your mother must be so proud of you," she told him.

Before she let Stan go, she found out who might be operating on Mom and who was in charge of her. She got a lot of details I never would've known anything about.

"You should've been that famous spy Mom calls you," I said to her after she shut the door on Stan.

"Mata Hari," Mrs. Buttermark said.

"She never said it in a mean way," I said, worried I might have hurt her feelings. "Mom loves you."

"Sweetie, it is the highest compliment to be called a Mata Hari. She was one smart cookie."

I took my jacket off and hung it on this thing called a hat tree. You have to be careful to make things like more than one jacket balance out or it falls over.

"Stan never told me half the stuff he told you."

"You can't expect to know what to ask," she said, helping me hang the jackets. Mom's opposite mine and Mrs. Buttermark's coat, that's how it had to be.

"Some things come with experience," she was saying. "Now my Harry was two times in the hospital before he—well, before he met his expiration date. I get the feeling your mother is in very good hands."

"Okay." I headed for the kitchen.

"Pour yourself a glass of milk and help yourself to anything else you want. Make a sandwich or heat up some of that bean soup in the container on the second shelf," she said as I looked into the fridge.

I was used to making myself at home with Mrs. Buttermark, and she did the same whenever she was in our apartment. We've been neighbors for as long as I could remember. Unless she's eating with me when Mom goes out, Mrs. Buttermark lives on soup and sandwiches. Food for kids and old ladies, she said once.

Except sometimes she makes meat loaf and mashed potatoes.

She went off to her room for a few minutes and I decided I wasn't in the mood for a sandwich. As I was putting the soup in the pot, she came back in jeans and a flannel shirt. When she wasn't doing the dressed-up look, Mrs. Buttermark dressed like Mom.

She goes to yoga class with Mom. She does Tai Chi, which is like karate, only a lot slower and without all the falling down. Mom says Tai Chi is too hard on her knees, that's why *she* doesn't do it—so most of the time Mrs. Buttermark doesn't seem like an old lady at all.

She turned the heat up and gave the soup a stir.

"I have to feed the fish," I said, remembering.

She turned the heat way down and said, "Let's go together."

I used my key but I was glad she came along. It was weird to go into our apartment knowing I'd be leaving in a few minutes. To know Mom wasn't coming home for a while. The fish hurried to the surface, like they'd missed me.

Mrs. Buttermark put water in an empty can so I could water the Christmas tree. She did the dishes we left in the sink. There were only two plates and glasses, forks and a frying pan. It didn't take long. I got my pajamas and toothbrush, and then we were outta there.

"Better stir the soup," Mrs. Buttermark said as we

crossed the hall again to her apartment. After she put a hot bowl of soup in front of me, she called somebody named Ben, who turned out to be a doctor. He knew a lot about broken legs, from the sound of things, and promised to make a couple of calls about Mom.

Then Mrs. Buttermark hung up and told me Ben would call over to the hospital and if there was anything we ought to know, he'd call us.

She clicked one fingernail on the counter, a sign she's thinking.

She called someone named Larry and told him what happened. I had no idea Mrs. Buttermark knew so many guys she called by their first names.

It's what I always suspected. People lead a whole life I know nothing about while I'm in school all day. Mrs. Buttermark asked me, "Where're the car keys?"

I shrugged. "Mom opened the car with them before she fell."

"Somebody from the supermarket mall probably picked them up," she said into the phone. "Or they're at the hospital."

She listened for a second.

She said, "Tell them you want her car parked over here in our building's lot. They can leave the keys with the superintendent. And if they don't have the keys, tell them the transmission is in perfect working order. We don't want it wrecked."

Mrs. Buttermark saw my eyebrows raise over this. She put her hand over the mouthpiece and said, "The people at the supermarket will think Larry is your mom's lawyer, which is probably a good thing."

When she got off the phone, I said, "Is he *your* lawyer?"

"I guess he would be if I needed one. He's my bridge partner." She put on water for tea. "Do you want some cheese and crackers to go with that soup?"

"Nah. It's good."

"Cheese and crackers are good too," Mrs. Buttermark said.

"I'm almost full," I said. "I might have room enough to squeeze in some apple pie." Mrs. Buttermark is never out of apple pie.

She put a slice of pie on a plate for each of us. We moved away from the counter to this little round table where Mrs. Buttermark looks out the window while she eats.

We looked at her Christmas tree too. It's small, but it's good. When I was little I loved all the tiny old-fashioned toy ornaments. There are pearly glass balls you can see yourself in, in miniature. Even the tinsel is extra-thin and short, so it doesn't hang down off the tree too far.

I'd begun to feel better, enough so that I had stopped worrying for a few minutes. I hoped that was okay.

"Ben hasn't called," I said.

"No news is good news," she said. She didn't look worried either.

"I guess so."

"What do you and your mom do on Saturday nights? Watch TV?"

"Play chess."

"Chess?"

"Yeah."

She put a hand on her hip. "All these years of living across the hall from you, how come I don't know you play chess?"

I shrugged. "Maybe because we play on a table in Mom's bedroom. The tabletop is the board and there's a drawer on each side for the pieces. We can leave it set up in there and it doesn't get messed up."

She was already on her way to the hall closet. I figured she was getting a jigsaw, because Mrs. Buttermark loves jigsaws. I don't exactly love them, but I don't mind sitting over them and sorting through the pieces when I'm with her.

She banged around in there for a minute and came up with a chess game. It was the kind with a fold-up board and plastic pieces, but who cares? It was a chess game.

One piece was missing, a bishop. Mrs. Buttermark got a tiny salt shaker to replace that piece and we were in business.

CHAPTER FOUR

I slept on Mrs. Buttermark's couch that night. I felt good when she turned out the lights. The couch was comfortable, even if my tailbone was sore.

Mrs. Buttermark told me that's what I hit when I fell. She did it herself one time. It could be sore for longer than Mom's leg was broken, but it would get better after a while. I fell asleep thinking it was funny that people had a tailbone.

Then I dreamed my mom got lost in the museum.

Also, she got off the subway train without me and I got lost. Then she fell into her cup of tea and drowned because I couldn't swim out to get her.

This was stupid because we don't have subway trains in Baltimore and no one drowns in a cup of tea.

I got lost in the museum once but I didn't even

know it. I had too many things to look at to wonder where Mom was. I was lost and I was found before I knew anybody was upset.

Anyway, I kept waking up all night long in a sweat to throw the blanket off. Then I'd wake up cold and huddle up under it again. The clock read 5:55 when I woke up the last time and used the bathroom.

Mrs. Buttermark got up a few minutes after I went back to the couch. I heard the shower running for a long time. I didn't see her again for an hour.

I have this idea the only way to live with a female is to be up ten minutes before she is so you can use the bathroom. Or don't even bother to get out of bed until an hour after she goes into the bathroom and shuts the door. It's true with Mom. It's true at Aunt Ginny's and Suzie's too.

You don't get anywhere till sometime past noon unless you absolutely have to be at school or karate class or a doctor's appointment. I don't know why.

I turned on a lamp and got one of the books off Mrs. Buttermark's shelf and started to read. It started off great, with a dead body on the second page, and this lady detective who decides to solve the murder.

* * *

We got to the hospital around eleven. For somebody who gets up way before the sun comes up, eleven is noon. I still felt like we made good time.

They had moved Mom to a different floor. After a few minutes of confusion, we found her room. She was sleeping, although her face didn't look so much like a mask.

There was a man standing on each side of her bed.

I could tell one of them was a doctor. White jacket, with a clipboard. He looked like a guy I saw on the basketball court in the park in summer. I hoped it wasn't really him, though, because that guy was in high school.

The other guy was dressed for a fishing trip, it looked like to me. He had an old face but his shoulders looked big, like he worked out. His white hair had been cut so short I could see pink skin underneath.

He looked strange. But there was a whiff of something in the room that made me want to take a deep breath.

The doctor asked us, "Are you family?"

"I'm Liz's neighbor," Mrs. Buttermark said to them as if she was the school principal. "This is Jake, her son. Who might you be?"

The doctor was quicker to answer, but he looked less interested than the other guy. The doctor said some things about how the swelling had gone down, so they could operate. Mom didn't have much pain, which sounded good to me.

The other guy turned out to be my granddad.

"Colonel Wexler," he said, and shook Mrs. Buttermark's hand. He didn't say anything to me. It was almost like he didn't know I was there.

From his voice, I always pictured him being something like the pictures of my dad, only older. I had the idea he wouldn't exactly surprise me if I ever met him.

He did surprise me.

My dad was blond, and taller than Mom in their pictures. Skinny too. Granddad was sort of chunky. If Mom was standing up, she'd be taller than him.

Granddad didn't look like a complete stranger. That was the amazing part. I guess he was thinking the same sort of things, because it was a few seconds before he shook my hand too.

He said, "Why don't we talk out in the hall and let Liz sleep? It was a long night."

We'd brought some things Mom might want. Mrs. Buttermark set the bag down by the window.

In the hall, I said, "The doctor said she slept all night."

"In and out," he said, looking only at Mrs. Buttermark. It was like he had something he wanted to say that I shouldn't hear.

With Mom and Aunt Ginny, I'd go away and let them say whatever they wanted to, but with Mom lying in that bed, I had to hear everything.

He said, "I got here around midnight, before they gave her more pain meds."

"So you came straight to the hospital," Mrs. Buttermark said. She was doing the same thing he did, talking over my head. I had the strangest feeling she was really talking to me. "Were you here all night? How very kind."

"That woman told me the boy was here by himself," he said.

The boy. Me? He meant me? I said, "Miss Sahara said I had to leave."

He glanced at me, then away. I'd seen that look before, only I couldn't think where. It made me feel like he thought I should've stood my ground or something. Be at the hospital when he got there.

I said, "I didn't know you were coming."

"Of course I came," he said, making me wish

Matthew's grandmother was on my side. He spoke in Mrs. Buttermark's direction, flicking a look over me. "You think I wouldn't come when you need me?"

"I didn't know Miss Sahara called you." That wasn't quite true. I did know, sort of. I suspected it, anyway.

"Liz should have called me herself," he said.

It happened I'd glanced at Mrs. Buttermark and I saw the look on her face. She didn't like what Granddad said. She kept quiet about it, so I did too.

Granddad went on saying, "That woman, Sahara, was, was—"

"Bossy," I said.

"So officious," Granddad said.

"Insufferable," Mrs. Buttermark agreed. I'd told her about Miss Sahara. "I guess she wanted to go home. It was probably the end of her day."

I hadn't thought of that.

"Liz and I were able to talk about how to handle her situation," Granddad said. I was glad to hear Mom had been awake sometimes. Maybe she'd wake up while I was here.

I could see Granddad had been an army guy his whole life. He sounded like he was in the middle of a war movie, deciding on his strategy. Not that I get to see a lot of those movies. Mom says I'm too young to watch stuff like that. Mainly it's that she doesn't like war movies. I get to watch movies that have drug addicts in them, and kissing. I'm too young for that kind of stuff too.

Granddad said a few more things about the doctor, how good he is at this kind of surgery, and finished up saying, "I told Liz I'd see to the boy."

I was tired of being called "the boy."

"I'm Jake," I said.

"Of course you are," he said, making his voice sound like Santa Claus. Hearty. "I know that."

His eyes flicked over me once more, and then I knew where I'd seen that look—on the new kids in class. They looked nervous and sort of eager in the same way. They nearly always said something stupid-sounding. The wrong thing, anyway.

"I know it must look strange to you," he said to Mrs. Buttermark, "that Jake and I don't know each other better."

"Please don't worry about the kind of impression you're making on me," she said. "It's not important."

"When my son died—Jake's father—" He had Mrs. Buttermark hooked now. Me too. "Liz didn't call me then either. It was some stranger on the phone."

"Oh, I see," Mrs. Buttermark said, putting a hand on his arm. "This took you back to such a painful time. I wonder if you know that the doctors sedated Liz right away. They had to pack her leg in ice to keep the swelling down. And of course Jake couldn't call. He didn't have your number. Neither did I."

"No, I didn't know that." He looked at me then, not that flickering thing but a real look. "Are there any other people you ought to call for your mother?" my granddad asked. "Anybody she'd call to come and visit her if she were awake to talk to them?"

"Yeah, but they aren't in town now."

"That would be Ginny and a friend, Suzie," Mrs. Buttermark put in helpfully. "Jake, what about work? Did your mother have a deadline to meet?"

"She takes a little time off for Christmas," I said. "I don't know if she's going to be here longer than that."

"When we get home," Mrs. Buttermark said, "we'll call her editor and let him know she might need an extension."

"By this time tomorrow, she'll make decisions of that kind for herself," Granddad said. He wasn't rude exactly, just awfully firm.

Mrs. Buttermark didn't back down. "I'm not so sure. If they don't operate until tomorrow—"

"They'll operate in an hour or so," Granddad said. "As it happens, the surgeon Liz needs is a personal friend of mine. When I called him, he came over to the hospital. His surgical nurse arrived a few minutes ago."

Mrs. Buttermark said, "That's a handy fellow to know."

He said, "We were in the service together. He's an old friend."

Mrs. Buttermark said, "I think your mom will want to see you before she goes to surgery, Jake. Why don't we all go sit by her bed?"

I nodded.

"Well, good you're here if Liz wakes up in the next few minutes," Granddad said. "I have to make a trip out to my car."

Mrs. Buttermark said, "You rented a car?"

"I drove up," he said. "It was a lot easier on the nerves than the sitting and doing nothing of taking a plane."

"A man of action," Mrs. Buttermark said, sort of like she admired that.

When he went outside, Mrs. Buttermark said we ought to check Mom's calendar at home. In case there were appointments that had to be postponed.

Mrs. Buttermark was in planning mode. "Everything you shopped for must be frozen solid by now," she said.

"Don't worry about it," I said. "At least we know the ice cream didn't melt."

She laughed and ran her fingers through my hair the way she does. The same way Mom does, which usually makes me feel like they like me. At that particular second, it made me wish somebody besides Mom could've fallen and broken their leg.

That old lady in the parking lot, maybe.

Which was a terrible thing to think, I know. Worse, I didn't even feel bad about it. I just wished it was Mom who was ruffling my hair.

CHAPTER FIVE

Some nurses were busy with Mom. They'd pulled a curtain around her bed, and when we came to the door, they told Mrs. Buttermark we'd have to wait.

We found a waiting room down the hall. Somebody had put this sickly little Christmas tree on the coffee table. It looked like they'd been taking it out of the hospital attic for about fifty years. All its shine had worn off.

Mrs. Buttermark's Christmas tree isn't new either, but hers looks like she means it. It looks cheerful and plump. Like somebody hopes Santa will come down the chimney, even after so many years of living in an apartment with no fireplace.

When Granddad came back, he carried a newspaper. He smelled like he'd been smoking. I sort of liked it. Mrs. Buttermark explained that we hadn't seen Mom and then said, "Ned, where are you planning to stay?"

"I haven't checked in anywhere yet."

"Liz has a sofa bed in the room she works in," Mrs. Buttermark said. "I think she'd like for you to use it."

It took me a minute to understand I wasn't going to spend that night on Mrs. Buttermark's couch.

The surgeon came down the hall then, and talked for a few minutes about the kind of broken leg people can get if their leg gets caught in a ladder while they're falling off it. Twisted.

It's the same broken leg people get from slipping underneath something when they fall. Twists are much worse than what he called a clean break. That's why they had to operate instead of just set the bone. Mom would have to exercise a lot as it got better. By next winter, she wouldn't know anything had ever happened to her leg, that's how fine she would be.

I said, "Can I see her?" because I knew I should. I didn't like the idea of talking to her knowing her leg was twisted.

"She's already prepped for surgery," the doctor said, which sounded like a no. "She's going to be good as new. There's no need to worry."

I got a sick feeling from being glad I couldn't see Mom sleeping that way again. It was probably another horrible thing to think, but I was already hoping I could wait until she woke up. The doctor left us.

Mrs. Buttermark asked Granddad a bunch of questions about where he lived in North Carolina. Mainly I found out he lived alone. And he was retired, like Mrs. Buttermark. I was glad she was there to figure out what to say to him.

Then we sat for a while and looked at magazines. There weren't many, and none of them were any good. Granddad turned to the crossword puzzle in the newspaper. Once in a while he asked Mrs. Buttermark for a word, but she never had a good answer.

Me either. I would've liked to know one to give him, but I couldn't even understand the clues. It began to seem like we'd been there all afternoon. I said, "How long has it been?"

Granddad looked at his watch. "Forty-eight minutes."

I wanted to groan. The doctor had said it would be about four hours before they had anything more to tell us.

Mrs. Buttermark said, "I'm going down the hall to find a restroom."

Granddad and I sat for a long while, probably a minute, until he set aside his crossword and said, "So what interests you?"

"I'm kind of a computer geek."

"These days, everybody your age is a computer geek."

I shrugged.

"What sport do you play?"

"I'm not too good at sports. That's why Mom got us to take karate."

I was starting to feel like Mrs. Buttermark, with no right answers. I knew Granddad was trying to make conversation and all, but maybe we could talk about the weather or something.

"So you don't play. What do you like to watch?"

"Watch?"

"On TV. You watch games, don't you?"

"Chess."

"Humph."

I gathered chess games didn't count. "And karate tournaments."

He leaned forward a little and said, "How about that kickboxing?"

"Master Kim says it lacks grace."

He sat back. "You don't say."

I could see this conversation was about to run downhill. I tried to remember anything Mom had ever told me my granddad liked or admired. "I'm a Republican," I said, because I think Mom once said he is.

This got a look.

Only a look. It was just as well. I had no idea what Republicans said to each other. The opposite of what Democrats say to each other, most likely, which was all *I* ever heard.

Since I agreed with almost everything I heard Mom and her friends say, I figured I'd told my granddad a lie. I could live with that.

"You get shoved around at school?"

"Not much, no."

"So how come your mother made you take karate?"

"She said I lived in my head too much," I said. "She said she does too, and it would be good for us."

"Karate," he said, like he'd have said "computers" when he was my age. Like he wasn't sure if somebody was making something up.

"She didn't *make* me take it. She gave me a choice. Karate, swimming, or tennis."

"So why'd you pick karate?"

I shrugged. "It sounds cool. Cooler than 'I can swim,' anyway." Besides, I don't like the water. Not that I was telling him.

I added, "And karate uniforms are cooler than white shorts." I'm not crazy about the idea of balls coming at me at fifty miles an hour either.

Maybe they're even faster than that, not that I want to know. There might be some life-or-death reason I'll have to play tennis someday, and really, that kind of information won't help.

"So how long you been voting Republican?" he said, and made me smile.

Mrs. Buttermark sat down with us then, and he went out to his car. He came back smelling like cigarette smoke again, so I figured that was why.

Mrs. Buttermark had it figured that way too. So after the second time, which was the third time if you counted the one before the doctor talked to us, she said, "I believe there's a smoking room near the lobby. You won't have to stand around in the cold."

"My dog's in the car," Granddad said. "I run him around the parking lot a few times to warm him up. Pretty sure he could just about freeze to death, the way that wind is whipping around."

"Oh, my," Mrs. Buttermark said. "I had no idea."

Granddad said, "Windchill must be brutal. I went down more often during the night."

"I mean," Mrs. Buttermark said, "I didn't know you had a dog out there."

"Me either," I said. "It's got to be awful cold." Like the basement where the elevator sits.

"Max. Goes everywhere with me."

"Well, he can't come in here," Mrs. Buttermark said. "Let's drive him over to the apartment, rather than let him suffer."

"He'll be fine," Granddad said in this gruff way. I was sure Mrs. Buttermark wouldn't argue with him.

She surprised me.

"*I* won't be," she said, "now that I know he's there. Put your jacket on, Jake. We'll be back here way before your mother comes out of surgery."

Granddad acted like Mrs. Buttermark was in charge of both of us. Maybe he really really wanted to get his dog in out of the cold, only he didn't know how to say so. If I was right, there was a kind of surprise in this.

I hadn't known Granddad long. He looked like a certain type of person, though, the type who can always say straight out what they want or how they think things ought to be. Like Aunt Ginny.

Somebody who felt shy about asking somebody to help him take care of his dog was not that type of person all the way through. He was more the type Mrs. Buttermark could boss around a little bit.

I spent the whole elevator trip to the ground floor reasoning this out. Over my head Mrs. Buttermark asked what kind of dog did Granddad have, and he said it was a Heinz 57.

Before I could ask if that meant a wiener dog, she said, "Max. Wonderful name for a dog," the way she does about a lot of things.

From some people this would seem to be the polite thing to say. Mrs. Buttermark always makes a person feel like she noticed them especially. Everybody I know who ever met her feels this way.

I didn't get all that cold walking through the parking lot. Granddad was right, though, that wind was whipping our scarves every which way. We had to pull them up over our noses to breathe.

Somehow, all these things came together to make me feel better, even though Mom was upstairs being operated on.

So it was a shock to see Granddad's dog wasn't the friendly kind. I mean, at first it huddled in the driver's seat looking cold and very small under a blanket. Like it was hibernating. I noticed it wasn't a wiener dog. It was silver-gray and bristly, like an allover mustache.

Then Granddad pushed the button on his keypad so the doors unlocked and that dog was up like a jack-in-the-box.

A crazy mad jack-in-the-box.

Okay, maybe there was an instant where it expected to see Granddad. Then it saw Mrs. Buttermark and me.

It went berserk. It barked and snarled like it had rabies or something, throwing itself at the window.

I yelped too, and fell against another car. Mrs. Buttermark grabbed me and held on. We both held on. I'm usually not afraid of dogs anymore, if they aren't too big. Especially since I'm taller than most dogs I meet now.

I got beaten up by a dog once, though.

Don't laugh. It wasn't funny.

That dog stood nose to nose with me at the time. It wanted to play some kind of dog game of run and bump each other. Like bumper cars with those big rubber bumpers that keep you from having a real crash. Except I was four and I didn't know about bumper cars yet.

I didn't have any bumpers either.

I had a babysitter who was busy looking at magazines in the park.

I got knocked over every time I got up to run away. I kept trying because I thought that dog might eat me if I stayed down. And every time I got up, that dog thought I was saying, *This is fun, let's do it again.*

It was a horrible nightmare of trying to catch my breath, wanting to cry or yell for help, and getting knocked over and losing my breath again. When I couldn't get up again, the dog came over and laughed in my face. That's how it seemed to me. Probably it was a dog's way of saying, *Good game, huh?*

That's when this older kid rescued me. He came over and shoved the dog away. When he pulled me up off the ground, he brushed me off and patted my shoulder and wiped my face with his sleeve. I kept on crying.

He said dogs like to play a bumper car game. He'd been throwing a Frisbee for his dog, only I must've looked like more fun. I remember him telling me all of this.

Looking back on it, I guess it was a brave thing he did. Not shoving the dog away. It was his dog, after all. Wiping a little kid's snotty face on his own sleeve was pretty brave.

He probably felt bad about the whole thing.

The babysitter told him it was nothing, I wasn't hurt, don't worry about it. Something like that. I was four, but even then I could see she thought he was cute or something. It was true, I wasn't really hurt, but I get nervous around dogs now.

This was not a dog to make you nervous. This was a dog to keep away from. Little, but mean. He was slobbering all over the window, trying to get to us. His teeth made little clicking noises on the glass.

"Better stand back," Granddad said to us.

Mrs. Buttermark and I were already backed up.

Granddad opened the car door and snatched at the dog's collar fast. The same way the lion tamer knows to snap the whip at the first sign of trouble. He grabbed the dog by his collar and picked him up like a little kid, holding him tight against his chest.

That dog quieted right down.

"He's been sick lately. We had to see a lot of vets, so he's anxious about strangers," Granddad said. "Probably feeling worse since he's so cold."

I didn't think that dog looked all that sick or even cold. Steam was coming off him. His breath showed on the air, of course. All our breaths showed on the air. But he had wispy little breaths of steam rising out of his bristly fur when he moved, I saw it.

He looked old and crabby, that's the type of dog he was.

He even looked at us with that same dog laugh that I remembered, except it didn't look much like, *Good game, huh?* It looked more like, *Scared ya bad, didn't I?*

I wondered where in the apartment he was going to be. Where I was going to be. Because I didn't want to be around him at all.

Mrs. Buttermark hadn't said anything, and neither had I. Granddad said, "He's a good little fellow. He won't tear anything up or chew on the furniture."

"I think Jake and I will take our car, and you follow in yours," Mrs. Buttermark said.

So that's what we did.

As we got into Mrs. Buttermark's car, I was thinking about how she sounded like that dog wasn't even horrible. Of course, that's Mrs. Buttermark's specialty, making other people feel like, don't worry, everything's working out.

"I don't like his dog," I said to her.

"I don't care for him either," she said. "I hope it didn't show. Did it show?"

I shook my head.

"Oh, good. Because I guess you saw what I saw," she said. "Your grandfather just loves that dog."

I nodded.

I've known Mrs. Buttermark a long time. Since I was two or three, anyway. Long enough to know that she was telling me in the very nicest way that no matter how much I didn't like that dog, this was the last chance I had to say so.

At least until Granddad went home.

"Let's look at him like a scientific subject, the way Suzie does," she said. "Each day, we'll notice something about him that's a good reason why your grandfather *would* love him."

I looked over at Mrs. Buttermark.

"We don't have to love him too, or even like him," she said. "We just have to find one reason why your grandfather does."

"Then what?" Because I didn't think that dog was going to be doing us the same favor.

"Then we'll pretend we're your aunt Ginny and reflect that to him."

Inside, where Mrs. Buttermark couldn't hear it, I groaned.

Aunt Ginny has this thing she does with people on the wilderness weekends. Especially the ones she doesn't like much. She finds something in them that is, for a moment at least, a good or interesting part of them, and reflects it at them. Like the way sunlight hits a mirror, that's the way she puts it.

She sees something she can like or admire and gives them her sunniest smile. She smiles from her heart. And by the end of the weekend, she says, she nearly always likes them. She says it's like a miracle is worked, not on them—on her.

I looked over the seat to make sure Granddad was behind us as we turned onto the avenue. "I wonder if a dog knows the difference."

Mrs. Buttermark said, "What difference?"

"Between giving him a sunny smile and baring our teeth at him."

Mrs. Buttermark laughed.

Aunt Ginny is nice. And smart. I love her and all. But she has some wacky ideas.

CHAPTER SIX

Granddad put his suitcase down, told his dog to sit—which the dog did—and looked around. It took me a minute to realize he wasn't crazy about what he saw.

We don't have the kinds of stuff I see in other kids' houses: plaid couches, curtains to the floor, and wall-to-wall carpet.

Nope.

Our place is more, like, amber beaded curtain between the living room and kitchen. No curtains at all at the windows because of so many plants on glass shelves.

Mostly everything else is brown or straw-colored because it's wood or leather or linen or, well, baskets. Even the rug on the floor is made of basket stuff.

Except Mom covered the couch with a bright quilt made from Indian fabrics with little mirrors sewn into it here and there. It has places where the fabric has worn through and you can see another strong color underneath. I could see how to Granddad's eyes, this still only looked worn out.

I was glad Mrs. Buttermark did the dishes. Our Christmas tree looked good, even though the lights were off. It even smelled like Christmas in here.

On the other side of the room, where most people would put a TV, we had the fish tank. A big saltwater aquarium. As long as the couch. Even plaid people usually forget about everything else and head straight for the fish tank. Granddad hardly noticed it.

I said, "The TV is in that cabinet."

"Fine, fine," he said.

"You can sleep in this room." I started down the hall. "Mom keeps sheets on the sofa bed, in case anyone ever needs to crash."

He followed me and the dog followed him. Mrs. Buttermark had said she'd run into her own apartment while I got Granddad settled. So I was trying to think of everything Mom said when people stayed over.

Granddad set his suitcase on the sofa bed. "Are there many crashers?"

"Aunt Ginny after she had surgery. Mrs. Buttermark last month. The guy in the apartment above hers had a leak in his bathroom and the water came into hers."

He unzipped his suitcase. Inside, it looked extremely neat. Everything sort of lined up, no matter that it was going to be a shirt shape or a sock shape once it was unfolded. I couldn't imagine how he'd gotten it to do that.

"I'm going to check the fish," I said.

I looked at our living room again. I saw some things that could bother somebody who packs in straight lines. Maybe it wasn't the beaded curtains at all.

I stacked up the magazines on the coffee table and made them line up with the edge. I went all around the room moving things into straight lines, even the easy chairs. Even the pillows Mom calls toss pillows, which she always does, *tosses* them onto the couch and chairs.

When I finished, the room looked strange to me. I had a feeling it would look better to Granddad. Then I fed the fish.

"It's been a long day," I told them as they nibbled at the surface of the water. "Mom won't be coming home again tonight."

I heard the sound of dog toenails on the floor. Granddad said, "This a hobby of yours?"

"Suzie's," I said. "She keeps her fish here with us because sometimes she's away for a couple of weeks at a time."

"I don't much care for keeping fish or birds," Granddad said. He sounded like he thought it ought to be a rule for everybody. "They don't seem suited to being pets the way cats and dogs are."

His dog leaned against his leg as they stood there. It made me think of the way I leaned against Mom when I was little. I doubted it was the same thing at all.

"These guys have a perfect life," I said.

"You think so?" Granddad's eyes kind of trembled. "I think they're missing a lot."

"The chance to get eaten by bigger fish?" I said, mostly out of surprise. Also, because I thought these fish had it good. Then I realized I sounded rude.

"There's nothing wrong with taking chances," Granddad said. "It's how we grow."

I didn't say anything.

"I mean, you don't have to do anything stupid. Risk is part of living a life, a full life."

"Mom doesn't like for me to take chances."

"Well, you have to do what your mother tells you," he said, looking away from me. "I don't mean to interfere."

He didn't sound sarcastic or anything when he said it. I didn't like to think he got the idea that I was a momma's boy. Aunt Ginny is always complimenting me and Mom that I'm really good at being a separate person.

A guy.

I didn't like how separate we were right now. I wasn't sure I liked Granddad either. It was good of him to come and get Mom operated on and all, but nobody needed him to criticize Suzie. She saved fish and birds from dying all the time.

Mammals too, like dolphins and whales. If it was cruel to keep these fish, she'd be the first one to set them free.

"So you were out at the supermarket when this happened," Granddad said, changing the subject. "I suppose that means the cupboards are bare."

"Nope." I led the way to the kitchen. "Mom plans ahead in case of getting snowed in or something. We never run out of eggs or spaghetti." The sound of dog toenails followed me, and so did Granddad.

"Now that surprises me," he said. "I don't remember her being someone who planned ahead."

"Yeah, well, some memories don't have anything to do with what's real," I said, more or less to myself.

Okay. I was saying it to him.

"That something your mother taught you?" he said, looking the kitchen over like he didn't like it much either.

"I figured that one out for myself," I said, looking at him the way he looked at the kitchen. I opened the pantry and reached for a jar of tomato sauce.

"Can't eat cooked tomatoes," he said. "Got any bacon? Milk or cream?"

"Maybe." I looked for the milk, mainly, because that's easy to run out of. Mom had heavy cream. She'd bought it to make whipped cream before Suzie left and then she never got around to it. I said, "It's old."

He checked the carton. "Expiration date is a week away. Cream lasts longer than milk."

"No bacon," I said, as he took the Parmesan cheese off the shelf.

"Here's smoked ham," he said. "Can we use that?"

"Sure." Do what you want, that's what I didn't say.

He put water to boil and then went through the cabinets, checking out weird stuff like marinated artichokes and roasted red peppers. Mom uses those now and then.

He found a jar of black olives with pits and some brown peas called capers and a can of anchovies. He kept making these little *umm, good* sounds, acting like all of it was buried treasure.

He sliced up a leftover piece of red onion, thin as paper, and used up the last of the lettuce, mixing it with some of the other stuff to make a salad that *he* looked happy with, anyway.

The dog came over near me and sniffed the air in my direction.

"He's starting to remember you," Granddad said.

"Remember me?"

"You were about a year old when I got him," Granddad said. "You were both puppies, crawling around on the floor. You used to try to pull his tail."

I waited to see how this made me feel. If it made me remember Granddad any better, since he did used to live in Baltimore. Mainly, it made me wonder if he was remembering some other grandson. One he might decide he liked better.

He stirred the spaghetti into the boiling water for a minute. He had me crack eggs into a big bowl while he sliced the ham into little slivers. He stirred the spaghetti again and mixed a whole lot of stuff together with the eggs—cream and ham and cheese.

He ground a lot of pepper into it. I decided against telling him I don't like pepper. "Did you learn to cook like this in the army?"

"Marines," he said. "There's a difference."

I figured.

I'd seen a couple of movies where guys from the navy and the army, or maybe it was the marines, got into big fistfights with each other, like they weren't all on the same team or something. I figured getting into fights with guys you could have been friends with was their idea of fun. I stopped worrying about reflecting at the dog so much. I needed to work on reflecting at Granddad.

Meanwhile, he called the hospital and found out Mom was still in surgery. That everything was going well. He had somebody's name who was supposed to answer these questions for him, which was more than I would've gotten. So I reflected that at him. I felt a little better. It was a start.

Granddad drained the spaghetti and put it into the bowl with the raw eggs, tossing the whole mess like crazy.

"We're eating raw eggs?"

"The heat of the spaghetti cooks them," he said. "The eggs make the sauce cling instead of floating around at the bottom of the bowl."

I hoped we had some oatmeal left, because this didn't look like my kind of food.

The doorbell rang.

It was Mrs. Buttermark with a big plate full of sandwiches, each one in its own ziplock bag. "I thought you fellas would like to have something to eat," she said, coming in. "Don't you love Liz's apartment? It's such a welcoming pla—"

She looked at me. I didn't say a word.

"My," Mrs. Buttermark said, which is what she says when the jigsaw piece looked perfect but it still didn't fit. She turned toward the kitchen. "I didn't realize you'd cook."

"You mean you didn't think I could," Granddad said. "Why don't you sit down with us?"

Mrs. Buttermark looked flustered. "I made all these sandwiches."

"Let's put them in the fridge," Granddad said. "We'll have a hot meal before we return to the hospital. The sandwiches will tide us over later."

I was glad she stayed. If she wasn't planning to go to the hospital with us, I'd've asked her to come along.

Granddad wasn't quite a stranger, okay. It wasn't like we were buddies either.

The holiday phone calls were never enough to make me feel like I got to know him. It was more like he was calling me on birthdays because he was supposed to. I never felt bad about this. It wasn't as if I called him, ever.

It looked like there was a good chance we'd get to know each other now. Probably we could take it slow. I mean, I had a place in me that was willing to be friends. To be family. It hadn't happened yet.

So it helped that Mrs. Buttermark stayed to eat spaghetti and the weird salad and make conversation easier. She filled Granddad in on Aunt Ginny, how Mom helped her through college after their parents died.

She talked about Suzie being part of our family and even bragged about my grades. I realized Mrs. Buttermark had become part of our family. She kept me from getting that uncomfortable feeling I didn't know Granddad well enough to feel like family.

The salad seemed exactly right to go with the spaghetti, which was very good. Not the way Mom makes spaghetti. But good. "We have to make this for Mom when she comes home," I said.

"Thank you," Granddad said. "That's quite a compliment."

"Would you look at that dog?" Mrs. Buttermark said.

We all did.

Granddad had put down a dish of smelly canned food for him when we sat down. I'd ignored the scraping noise he made pushing the dish around while we ate.

He was sitting at attention next to the empty dish. More than empty, it looked like he'd polished it. A job well done, he seemed to be trying to say.

"Such a little man," Mrs. Buttermark said as if she couldn't be more proud of him.

He *was* sort of well-behaved-looking. Like he'd never thrown himself against a car door. Like it wasn't his saliva that was dripping onto the window when he did.

I tried not to think too much about how tricky a dog he might really be.

By the time we'd cleaned up the kitchen and were ready to go, the dog had been all over the apartment, sniffing everything. Everything.

For an old dog, he was pretty athletic. He could

hop up practically everywhere my cat could get before she died, like the tabletops, although he hopped up on a chair first. He'd even taken a drink of water from the fish tank, the way my cat used to do.

The fish didn't seem to mind too much, so I decided not to care. Even though he had a perfectly good bowl of water in the pantry. We left the door open for him so he could get to it.

This was a new place for him to get used to and all, so I could sort of understand it when he tried to leave with us. Granddad let me get out in the hallway with Mrs. Buttermark, then called the dog back.

He went, head down, a dog in trouble. It was halfway cute, if you like that sort of thing. If you didn't know he could turn into a nightmare dog. Granddad came out into the hallway. As he tried to shut the door, the dog tried to get out.

Granddad opened the door, walked inside, the dog followed. "Stay."

This time Granddad stepped out more quickly, shutting the door.

The dog threw himself against the door, barking. Nightmare dog. It was different this time, though. It was a whiny bark. Probably no saliva dripping down the door.

"No," Granddad said in that gruff voice, without opening the door.

The dog stopped throwing himself. He stopped barking. I could hear him whine, though. He sounded really pitiful. I'd never thought of a dog having feelings quite like mine. This one was sad.

Mrs. Buttermark looked like she was about to offer to stay behind. She looked at me first, and I let her see I needed her to come with us. I didn't even mean to. I felt bad for the dog.

Granddad could stay behind, that's how I felt. He wouldn't, though. He was coming to the hospital with me and Mrs. Buttermark. The dog had to be able to take it, that's all there was to it.

"I won't be gone long," Granddad said, looking at the door. Something in his voice had changed. I could see he felt awful about leaving the dog there alone.

He also looked embarrassed to be talking to his dog like that. I couldn't love the dog the way Granddad did. Even if it was sad and halfway cute. I used to talk to our cat. Apparently, I used to pull this dog's tail.

"You won't be cold here," I said to the door. "You have the fish to keep you company. If you get yourself a drink, try not to lap any of them up. Especially the little brown one that can puff itself up. I think it's poisonous."

Nothing from behind the door.

The dog stayed quiet as we practically tiptoed toward the elevator. Mrs. Buttermark ruffled my hair.

I felt like a complete idiot.

CHAPTER SEVEN

Half the afternoon had passed while we were eating spaghetti. Hours didn't seem to stretch as far as they usually did.

Mrs. Buttermark said we had to stop for flowers. Also, this little Christmas tree she called Rosemary. Granddad kept nodding, like he was glad Mrs. Buttermark took charge.

I started to worry about seeing Mom. I hoped she'd be the same as usual, with her leg in a cast. I knew she would be in bed and operated on. If she was awake, I figured I could take it. If she wasn't moaning. I wanted to see her, of course, but also I wanted her to be feeling fine.

Partly because I hadn't seen her feeling fine since we started across the parking lot the day before. And partly because I knew surgery had this way of changing things. Aunt Ginny had gone into surgery last year and came home missing a part. I didn't miss it. I hardly noticed. But she seemed to miss it.

When we got in the car, there wasn't much space for me on the backseat. Mrs. Buttermark had taken her knitting, which weighed a ton. I know, because I offered to carry it for her. Mrs. Buttermark had even packed a few of Mom's things in a little suitcase.

Mom was in surgery when we got there, the way Granddad said she would be. He carried a book. I was the only one who wasn't prepared to sit around the hospital awhile.

I found out why Mrs. Buttermark bought so many flowers. She took the hospital's awful little tree to the restroom, where maybe she threw it away. Or maybe it looked better in the restroom.

In the waiting room, she arranged three pots of Christmas flowers with this watering thingy. I read on the package that it would keep them watered for three weeks. That left Rosemary and a bushy plant with tiny red flowers for Mom.

Then I saw why her knitting weighed so much. She'd brought magazines for the waiting room. Good ones, if you were Mom or Aunt Ginny or even Suzie.

There were two *Smithsonian*s in there. I looked at those for a while.

Granddad closed his book with a loud pop.

"Not enjoying it?" Mrs. Buttermark asked him.

"Too many references to computers and I don't know enough about them," Granddad said. "Pass me that *Smithsonian,* if you've finished with it, Jake."

The doctor found us looking sort of like we had moved in, reading and knitting and all. "Everything went better than I expected," he said. "She's in recovery. You can see her soon."

I liked the sound of that.

He said, "She'll be woozy. She's not in pain. We'll keep her comfortable."

Granddad said, "How long before she comes home, Dave?"

It took me a second to realize he was talking to the doctor. I know doctors have first names, of course, just I never called one Dave or anything that didn't start with "Doctor."

He answered the same way. "Ned, she'll be home inside a week. Best I can do."

I glanced at Mrs. Buttermark and caught her glancing at me. I figured she heard that *best I can do* the same way I did. It was the best he could do to get

Granddad off the hook of babysitting for me as fast as possible.

He was going on to say other stuff, though. "She'll use crutches for several weeks. You might arrange for a wheelchair for the first month."

A wheelchair. Okay. Then crutches. Double okay.

In my mind, Mom was getting better.

The doctor said by next winter Mom would never know this happened. I did the math on that. We were about two months into winter this year, which left ten months till next winter. It seemed a long time to wait.

A tiny thought fell out of the back of my mind. Joey and I would make a contest of who could get down the hallway fastest on the crutches. I'd have plenty of time to learn how to do wheelies in the wheelchair. I could picture Mom cheering me on.

The doctor promised to call Granddad the next morning, give him a report. An update, he called it. And the whole picture fell apart. I knew Mom would get better, but we had a ways to go first.

A nurse came to stand nearby and the doctor went off with her. That left us sitting in the waiting room again. Granddad went out for a smoke.

I said to Mrs. Buttermark, "Granddad's in a hurry to go home."

I expected her to agree, but she said, "Why do you say that?"

"He told the doctor he wants Mom to go home as soon as she can."

"We all want that."

"I know. I think Granddad doesn't want to take care of me."

"I think he wants what's best for you, Jake."

"I know, I know. He also wants to go home."

Mrs. Buttermark looked at her magazine, and after a moment said, "I really didn't get that feeling at all."

Granddad got back a few minutes later. He brought a handful of comic books for me and a newspaper for himself. I was set for an hour or so, and Granddad turned to the crossword puzzle.

Mrs. Buttermark came right out and asked him, "What do you usually do with yourself at this time of year, Ned?"

"I have a few buddies," Granddad said, and then upped the volume to that hearty voice he used about swimming. "We order in ham sandwiches and cranberry sauce from a local restaurant. Sing a few carols if the mood hits us. Biggest poker game of the year."

"Does it bother you to miss it?"

"Not a bit." This was also a hearty voice, but not at all the same. This time, he really meant it. "I can play poker anytime."

Mrs. Buttermark grinned at me.

"The Christmas flowers look really good," I told her.

"Yes, you've made a real improvement," Granddad said. "That tree was depressing."

We didn't get to see Mom for over an hour. Her leg was propped up in this little hammock that hung from the ceiling, and her hair was a flattened mess. But she looked pink and not too tired out.

I grinned the second I saw her. This was even better than wheelies.

Mom hugged me and called me "beautiful boy," like I was still little. It was a little embarrassing in front of Granddad. I figured she'd been taking medication and all.

"Ooh, little Christmas tree," she told Mrs. Buttermark, and sniffed at it. "Mmmm. Rosemary." I figured the tree had its name on the tag or something.

We made up a list of everything else she wanted us to bring. Mrs. Buttermark had been calling Granddad Ned, and he called her Donna. Mom noticed this and wiggled her eyebrows at me. I felt good, seeing that. Mom had to be feeling pretty well.

A nurse came by and told us we had to go. Mom was supposed to go to sleep. We said okay, and then we talked for a few more minutes. Mom asked if the TV on the wall worked.

So I thought maybe that meant she didn't expect to pass out the second we left. I mean, she never just goes to sleep. I thought maybe it would be like the doctor said, she'd be woozy. She wasn't.

The TV didn't work.

"Mrs. Buttermark brought some magazines," I said. "Would you like to have a couple of those?"

"Magazines would be great."

"I'll go get them," Granddad said.

"I just remembered," Mrs. Buttermark said. "About your work. Should we call anyone?"

"Not yet," Mom said. "If I have to be here more than another couple of days, I'll figure something out. Borrow Ginny's laptop, maybe, so I can work in this bed."

The nurse came by again and shooed us out. I think Granddad was a little bit glad. Probably he was worried about his dog. His nightmare dog.

"Ned," Mom called as we were leaving. "Thank you for coming so quickly."

Granddad said, "Dr. Dave expects you to run a marathon next week, that's how fast you're going to be up and around."

CHAPTER EIGHT

It had started to snow a little. No one said, *Oh, no, snow on top of the ice.*

There would probably be more people who slipped and fell tomorrow morning. Halfway home, a fire engine passed us, and I didn't wonder where it was going. I wondered if I had been falling asleep.

We passed Christmas lights, but we didn't say, *Look how pretty.*

We hardly said a word in the car. Except for the kinds of things people say in winter, like, "It'll warm up in a minute."

Also the kinds of things people say after they see a person who had surgery. "She looks good." Of course they could say the opposite if that were true, they just wouldn't say it in front of me.

Mom did look good. She looked like she had a

broken leg. She looked regular, like I'd hoped. I didn't have to be scared about her anymore.

I felt like Granddad had his dog on his mind, now that we were on our way home. I figured that was a good thing. Like knowing Mom would be thinking about me.

Parking his car, I noticed our car was there. It was too cold to look to see if our groceries were in there. "Nothing that can't wait till morning," Granddad said.

Mrs. Buttermark said, "We're all tired," and we were.

We had to walk around the side of the building where it stayed shady most of the day. Granddad took Mrs. Buttermark by the arm as we picked our way over the snow-covered icy spots.

"Remind me to buy a sack of salt," Granddad said.

Mrs. Buttermark knew as well as I did that the super had dropped a truckload of salt on this side of the building. We were too pooped to say so.

In the summer, Mr. G would complain about how the salt messed up the blacktop. He'd paint over it with something that smelled like tar. That's what Mrs. Buttermark said it smelled like, anyway. Some days this could've been a conversation. But no one said a word until we were saying good night in the hallway.

Mrs. Buttermark opened her door and found Mom's car keys hanging on the inside doorknob. "Mr. G came by," she said, and gave them to me as she said good night.

Granddad opened our door. The dog had waited there for us. I thought he might have heard us coming. Granddad put his hand on the carpet. "Feel here," he said, with a voice like a bear.

It was warm. The dog had stayed there, sleeping maybe, but stayed there the whole time we were gone. Granddad looked like this meant he was quite a dog, and I made up my mind to reflect this right back at him. Sooner or later, Mrs. Buttermark would ask what I was reflecting to that dog.

"I'm going to walk him," Granddad said as I was taking off my jacket.

"I'll go with you." I zipped my jacket up again.

"Not necessary." He didn't act mad. More like he was saving words. Maybe he sounded that way on a mission in wartime. He wore a black zippered jacket that made me think of movies like that.

"He has to get used to me," I said.

I had to get used to him too.

And I had to try to notice something Granddad

liked about his dog. Something more than he could keep the carpet warm. I thought it might not count as such a compliment. The dog didn't want to be in the apartment when we left, and maybe behind the door was as far away as he could get. If he had a choice, he might have been happier waiting in the car.

The other thing I was thinking, I had to get used to the way Granddad talked in that gruff voice. Maybe I had to try to find something I liked about him. Not the stuff he was doing that we needed him to do. Something I just liked, period.

And maybe I had to give Granddad something he could like about me. I didn't want him to feel like I wasn't even trying to like his dog. Maybe that was the place to start.

I thought about what I liked best about Joey Ziglar's dog: it hardly noticed me. People were holding the leash or the food, or they weren't, that's all.

The dog sat down in the elevator, the way well-trained dogs do, and then stood up again. Then he sort of checked in with Granddad with a glance. This was a dog that paid attention to people.

"Your dog looks smart. This kid I know, Joey Ziglar? His dog doesn't look that smart."

I felt bad right away. I decided I'd tell Joey I said this and why, then I wouldn't feel like such a crummy friend. Besides, Granddad did perk up a little.

He said, "Max is smart."

"I guess you have to walk your dog a lot."

"Max."

"Right. Max."

The dog sat down like he thought he had to obey the rules. But he didn't look happy for the two seconds until the elevator stopped and the door opened. I figured the floor was too cold for sitting, even with a furry butt.

Joey Ziglar's dog could be described as four legs that needed to be walked. And then it slept until the next walk or until somebody put food in its dish. I got along fine with that dog.

I said, "Joey Ziglar has a dog that has to be walked about five times a day or it pees on the rug."

"Max won't do that."

"I wasn't worried about that," I said as we went through the lobby. "Joey's dog is really old."

"Max is old," Granddad said. "Just not that old."

I had to hand it to Mrs. Buttermark. Always saying the right thing was not the easiest thing in the world to do.

"How many times do you walk him?"

"Four, five times. Six. It's good for me, the exercise."

I decided to drop the subject.

It was even colder outside, of course. It seemed colder than when we'd been out here ten minutes before. There was no question of sitting. The dog took quick short steps, as if he also hoped we wouldn't have to be out here too long.

Snow covered everything like sugar on a cookie, so I stayed away from the places that were shadiest during the day. Lucky for us, the dog wasn't in the mood to walk around much. He peed on a telephone pole, a garbage can, and a tree that was stuck in a small square of frozen dirt. When the dog started pulling Granddad back to our building, we went.

"There's a park with a dog run near here," I said as we took the elevator. "I can show you tomorrow."

"Do you want one of those sandwiches Donna left in the refrigerator?"

"Not really." It was strange. I wasn't getting hungry the way I usually did. It was like my stomach had too many other things to worry about. Surgeries and stuff.

Granddad had his own key now, but he still

waited for me to unlock the apartment door. He was polite that way. I helped Granddad open the sofa bed and found the comforter for it.

The dog watched us from the corner of the room.

I wanted to go to bed. I'd begun to worry about walking around never knowing when the dog might go into nightmare mode. Besides, I wanted to prop my leg on a few pillows and see how Mom was doing. I got the extra pillows from her bed.

When I was in my pajamas, I went to tell Granddad good night. He had given the dog some leftover spaghetti and he was lighting up a cigarette.

I had forgotten about him smoking earlier in the day.

"You can't smoke in here," I said.

I might have liked it if he did. He smoked Camels. It was out of my mouth before I thought about it. Before I let myself like the smell of the smoke.

"Mom doesn't even let Aunt Ginny smoke in here. You could go through the kitchen window and sit on the fire escape. That's what Aunt Ginny does."

Except I'd never seen Aunt Ginny do it in the middle of winter.

While it was snowing.

That's what Granddad did. No complaint. He

climbed outside and brushed off a snow-covered metal step so he could sit down. Then he stood up.

For a minute there, I wasn't even worried about him liking me. I wondered if I was wrong to make him follow Mom's rules. Not just wrong—rude. I felt like I ought to stick my head out there and tell him, never mind, Mom would never know if he did it this once. Only I couldn't. It seemed more important to follow Mom's rules than ever.

The dog had finished the spaghetti. He kept licking the plate so it went sliding around on the floor near the window. Mom never let our cat eat out of our dishes, so this was probably a broken rule too.

I didn't know what Mom would have done if she was here, if she would have let Granddad smoke in the kitchen. I didn't know why he couldn't have thought of it while we were downstairs with the dog. Outside I could have liked that smoke smell for as long as it lasted.

The whole thing sort of irritated me.

Besides, how soon would the dog figure out there wasn't any more flavor on that plate? What if he turned into nightmare dog? I went to bed before Granddad came inside. I figured if he wasn't missing his poker game before, he was missing it now.

When he passed my doorway, he stopped and said, "Anything you want to talk about, Jake?"

I shook my head. I noticed the dog sat down behind him, sort of waiting for him.

"Your mom's going to get over this. You know that, don't you?"

"I know. It's weird she isn't here."

"It won't be long," Granddad said. "A few days."

I could see how hard he wanted to say the right thing. He *had* said the right thing, even if it didn't make me feel better. All of a sudden, I knew the right thing to say too. "I'm glad you're here."

He sort of crinkled up around the eyes when he smiled. He didn't look like somebody who ever sounded gruff. I guess Mrs. Buttermark had him figured out faster than I did.

Granddad got into bed after brushing his teeth, because I heard the bedsprings. I heard the dog jump up on the bed. Granddad told him "Shhh," even though he hadn't made a sound other than the jump up.

I wondered if Granddad thought it was against the rules to have his dog sleep next to him. I didn't think it was. Our cat slept in our beds. I got allergic to cat hair after a while.

Granddad fell asleep as soon as his head hit the pillow. At least that's when the snoring began. I sat up.

Mom has a whole ritual that goes with falling asleep. She brushes her teeth, she makes tea, she puts on bed socks. She collects stuff she wants to read but doesn't have to translate no matter what language it's in. She gets into bed and maybe an hour later, or two, her light goes out.

Or not. Sometimes I get up in the middle of the night and turn it out.

So. It was really possible for people to fall asleep the minute their head hit the pillow. Mom wasn't one of those people, and neither was I. The snoring got louder, like Granddad was falling even deeper into sleep.

He hadn't turned out the light. I tiptoed to the end of the hall and peeked in. The dog was curled up next to Granddad. He knew I was coming because his head was already lifted off his paws. As soon as he saw me, he showed his teeth.

I ducked away from the door. I went to my room and wrote Granddad a note. I left it on my bed where he'd be sure to see it.

I knocked on Mrs. Buttermark's door. She opened

it right away, dressed regular. I didn't have to feel bad about waking her up, because I hadn't.

"I'm sleeping over here tonight," I said, and she opened the door wider.

When we were sitting at her little round table having apple pie and hot chocolate, I said, "I can't sleep if I'm going to have to worry about getting up to use the bathroom in the middle of the night and being attacked because I forgot for a minute that dog was there."

"You wouldn't forget," Mrs. Buttermark said.

"True." I looked at her. "I wouldn't get to the bathroom alive either."

"You're sure your granddad will see the note?"

"Absolutely."

"I'm glad to have your company, Jake. I'm a little unraveled after seeing your mother that way."

Sometimes Mrs. Buttermark talks like she's a sweater. When she does, I try to do that too. I said, "I'm full of knots myself."

She smiled. "What shall we do to untangle?"

I looked out the window and saw snow falling around the streetlight. "An old movie, I think."

I slept on her couch that night, and Mrs. Buttermark slept in her recliner. The TV was still on when we woke up the next morning. A different movie was on.

It was dark outside. I could tell it was morning from the sound of cars warming up. "It's a school day," I said, remembering. "Today's the Christmas party."

I didn't care that much about the Christmas party, I wanted to say. I cared last week. This weekend had changed things.

"Go tell your grandfather I'll make breakfast," Mrs. Buttermark said, sitting up in her chair. "I'll shower and make pancakes."

Our apartment door opened as I stepped into the hallway. Granddad had the dog on the leash. I had a sudden worry come over me. What if he was mad that I'd moved across the hall?

I forgot all about school and said, "Mrs. Buttermark says she'll make pancakes as soon as she gets out of the shower."

"We can buy pancakes by the time she's out of the shower."

Obviously he'd noticed this thing about females and bathrooms too. "She'd probably like that."

"Get dressed," he said. "You can show me that park where I can walk the dog."

"Okay."

"Meet me downstairs."

Granddad had already showered. Steam had escaped from the bathroom and was rolling in the air of the hallway. I pulled my jeans on and my jacket. Wrapped a scarf around my neck. That's when I remembered I hadn't mentioned school. But there was plenty of time to get there; breakfast came first.

I caught up with Granddad and the dog at the tree where he had peed the night before. He didn't even bark at me. Actually, I think he ignored me.

As we started out, Granddad walked so fast, I had to trot to keep up. The dog had such short legs he would've had to trot to keep up with *me*. He ran alongside Granddad. So I could see how Granddad had kept him from freezing the day before. I thought maybe I'd warm up in a minute too.

The sky had begun to go gray. It didn't have the look of a day that would be sunny later. "Maybe more snow," Granddad said, also looking at the sky.

I didn't answer. My teeth were chattering unless I bit down. I wished I'd put a sweater over my pajama top before I put my jacket on. Too late now.

We got to the park pretty quickly. A lot of people were already walking their dogs. "I'll take Max through the park," Granddad said, digging into his hip pocket. "You go into the McDonald's there and order seven pancake breakfasts. No coffee. Donna will make coffee."

"She'll make tea."

"Get one black coffee. Large." He gave me the money to pay. "You wait inside. I'll be back in a few minutes."

"The dog run is over that way," I said, pointing.

"Go on," Granddad said. "Get inside and warm up."

CHAPTER NINE

I didn't have to go to school.

I didn't even have to ask if I could stay home.

"I think it's more important for you to see your mother today," Granddad said. We ate in our kitchen, where he passed bits of sausage to the dog. Max. There was some talk about how to manage Christmas, since Mom wouldn't get home in time for it.

Then Granddad said, "Anything special you're hoping to find under the tree, Jake?"

I shrugged, a small hope lighting up once more. "A bike."

"You've outgrown your old one?"

"I never had one. It's what I ask for every year."

Mrs. Buttermark kept her eyes on her plate, like eating pancakes was serious business. Granddad had some strong notions about risk. I hoped he wouldn't be mad that Mom never got me a bike. But if he got me one, Mom would probably have to let me ride it.

And when she saw I *could* ride it—I'd been riding Joey's for a year—and that I'd never ride in the street, she'd probably feel like it wasn't that scary after all.

She might even feel bad she'd never gotten one for me before. I had this little picture in my mind, me shrugging and saying, *That's okay. Mom.*

While I helped Mrs. Buttermark rinse off the pancake boxes for recycling, Granddad asked me what school I go to and looked up the phone number. While I finished getting dressed, he talked to the principal. Just like that.

I didn't know someone could call and get him on the phone. I thought the office ladies kept people from talking to him. Sort of the way the Secret Service protects the president from just any old person who wants to strike up a conversation with him. I'm not sure Mom ever talked to the principal.

Granddad made a couple more calls. Nothing to do with a bike, that I could tell. Mrs. Buttermark went over to her apartment, saying she'd make some fresh sandwiches for us to take over to the hospital.

Visiting hours at the hospital wouldn't even start

until two o'clock. We didn't have the excuse of Mom being in surgery so we could show up earlier. I didn't know what Granddad and I would do with each other all morning.

Still, it was sort of cool to miss school on a Monday, even if it was the day of the Christmas party. I fed the fish. They were always hungry.

"Well, that's taken care of," Granddad said, hanging up the phone. "It's early yet. I saw a YMCA in town. What say we go for a swim?"

"I can use the trampoline or something," I said, putting down the fish food. "Run a few laps, maybe."

"A swim," Granddad said as if I hadn't heard him. "Heated pool. Warm, rough towels."

I had skipped the shower. Now that I thought about it, I guess I'd skipped the shower since Friday.

I said, "I don't go in the pool, usually." Ever. I was sort of floundering here. I wanted him to know I wanted to do things together, just not the pool. "I'll shower if you're worried about it."

"Why won't you go into the pool?"

"I'll go in," I said. "Nobody drowns in the shallow end."

"You don't swim?"

"I *can't* swim," I said, getting annoyed with the way he made me sound uncooperative or something. Suzie offered to teach me to swim, and when I said no, that was the end of it.

Well, she asks again every so often, but she doesn't make a big deal out of it.

Granddad said, "Even nonswimmers can get some benefit from a pool. Exercise. I've got an extra cap."

I didn't have any idea what he was talking about. Who would do jumping jacks or push-ups in a pool, especially if they didn't swim? And those caps, pressing on my head until it felt like an overfilled balloon.

"I get embarrassed," I said. Granddad didn't seem to get it. He looked like he had half an idea I could swim but didn't want to.

The thing is, for the first time in my life, I really *wished* I could swim. It was plain to me that Granddad thought very highly of swimming. He might not care about tennis, and he didn't care one way or the other about karate. Swimming mattered.

"Try this on," he said. "It might be a little big for you."

When he offered me the cap, I took it. It looked

pretty cool, black with a blue zigzag like lightning. I pulled it on. It was a little big, which meant I didn't feel like my head would explode.

"Fine," I said. "If it'll make you happy, I'll come flap around in the shallow end."

"You can't learn to swim in the shallow end."

"I didn't know that," I said. I didn't believe it either. Where else would somebody learn? Or what was the shallow end for?

But he wasn't saying this like it was true. He was saying it like he'd be embarrassed if I stayed at the shallow end.

"You don't swim," he said, almost to himself. Then he looked straight at me. "That's why you don't go into the pool?"

"That's why a lot of people don't go into pools," I said. Okay, I yelled. A little. "I wouldn't want to learn in the deep end, that's for sure."

He looked at me as if I was one of Mrs. Buttermark's jigsaw puzzles. "Let's go," he said, and put out his arms for the dog to jump into them.

"You're not going to do one of those stupid throw-me-in-the-pool things, are you?" I asked him. "I don't have to go with you." It had been a rough weekend. I didn't want to top it all off by drowning.

"I wouldn't do that to you," he said. For a moment I thought maybe I hurt his feelings. He made his voice real hearty to say, "You don't have to get in the pool. Good thing about not being a swimmer, you'll never be a navy man."

I guess that was a joke.

CHAPTER TEN

We brought in the frozen groceries. Some of it went into the freezer. Lettuce and bananas had to be thrown away. A cracked jar of applesauce, that had to go too. Otherwise, everything could be eaten.

I took the cookies with us. I figured it was like the things we left in the sink, they'd defrost.

The dog stayed with Mrs. Buttermark. She'd suggested it and Granddad agreed. This would be easier on Max than being alone for hours at a time.

We also put most of her sandwiches in my backpack. Frankly, after four pancakes, I didn't think I'd ever eat again. Mrs. Buttermark had eaten three. And Granddad ate the rest. It surprised me he could think about sandwiches. If he got in the pool, he might not even float.

When we got to the Y, Granddad checked his watch

against the clock on the wall. "I'm going swimming," he said, in the tone of, *if you want to change your mind . . .*

I didn't say a word. The rubber swim cap was in my jacket pocket, stiff from the cold. I didn't even look at Granddad, so maybe he'd think my eardrums were frozen.

He said, "Want to meet back here in ninety minutes?"

I nodded.

"Just so I don't have to worry, you won't leave the building?"

"I'll go jump on the trampoline," I said, trying to sound like I had regular stuff I did at the Y. Instead of coming to a birthday party here once.

The party would've been great except there was always a long line at the trampoline. Nobody could jump for more than one minute at a time, in case they'd eaten too much cake and ice cream. And after cake and ice cream there was nothing else they'd let us do.

Granddad and I nodded little nods at each other like we were each going out on separate missions. Then we climbed the stairs together.

It was probably two minutes before we got to a place to turn in different directions. We didn't say a word the whole time, like we were already in different hallways.

It turned out the trampoline room is locked if there aren't a few kids around. I was the only kid. The guy wouldn't unlock the door.

I wandered around for a while. Some old guys were taking a yoga class. Some other people were studying or something, all sitting quietly in a classroom, reading. Nothing too interesting.

There were plenty of guys using the gym. Kids weren't allowed in there. I put on my shorts and ran around the track twice, until I found out kids weren't allowed in there either. At least not by themselves.

I didn't mind. I hadn't paced myself, like the rest of them were doing. I was getting ragged by that time. This last guy who chased me off said, "Why don't you go down to the pool?"

So I headed for the pool.

Granddad was not the only swimmer. He *was* the only one who swam like he was cutting through the water, using his arms for scissors. He went from one end of the pool to the other three times while I watched and didn't look like he'd be stopping anytime soon.

He was too busy to notice me.

I pulled the swim cap on and took my sneakers off.

A swimmer heaved himself up on the edge of the pool, a little breathless. "Can I go in to swim in my track shorts?"

"Sure. Leave your other stuff in one of the lockers."

So I flapped around in the shallow end for a while. I noticed there's a bar running along the side of the pool. I held on to the bar and pulled myself along to the deep end.

Not to the deepest part of the deep end, but definitely where I could've drowned if I lost hold of the bar. Well, except that there was a lifeguard watching.

I didn't feel like I was in danger, just that I didn't want to embarrass myself by needing to be rescued, or even helped. I didn't want to embarrass Granddad either.

After he swam the pool about nine more times, he slowed down and swam over to me. "That's it," he said. "Get comfortable with it."

"I don't need to learn to swim," I said, pulling myself along. I was headed back for the shallow end.

"Nah, nobody falls out of boats much anymore. Or into rivers. That sort of thing used to happen more often in the old days," he said. Then he laughed and said, "When I was a boy."

"I know those aren't the old days."

"Oh, they are," he said. "Don't kid yourself. The way things are going, you won't get as old as me before people will be calling today 'the old days.'"

That didn't sound too good.

He'd moved around in front of me and then stopped. I stopped pulling so I wouldn't bump into him. I flapped my feet around a little, like a swimmer does. I kept a tight grip on the bar. "Why didn't you ever come visit us?"

Granddad looked around the pool for a minute.

"At first I missed your father too much. And even before that, I'd forgotten how good it feels to be needed," he said. "Not that your mother ever needed me."

He looked embarrassed, same as when he was talking to his dog through a door. "I know that doesn't sound like much of a reason."

I got this feeling, like when his dog didn't want to stay in the apartment alone. Like I had to say *something*. "Our cat died last year," I said. "Mom and I miss her too much to get another one."

"Well. Probably you ought to give another cat a chance."

"We do. About every month we go to the pound

and look, especially at the kittens." Looking at the kittens was Mom's idea. It made me miss our cat more. "We don't feel like getting one."

"You *will* want one someday," he said. "It will just come over you."

"I guess."

What came over me at the pound, though, was wanting my old cat. I didn't want some new cat doing the things my cat didn't get to do anymore, like stick her paw in the fish tank. Or lie in the sun behind Mom's plants. Or curl up on my pillow. Even if it did make me sneeze.

The feeling I had, and really I knew it was thinking about my cat that did it, I wanted some peace and quiet while I messed around in the pool. I didn't want to miss my cat. Or Mom, even for a little while. Not that I was going to say so. It feels rotten, missing them.

"It's different with me, though," Granddad said after we'd had maybe a minute of peace and quiet. "You're not a kitten. You're my grandson. I'm your only grandparent."

I didn't mean to make him feel rotten too. I tried to let him off the hook. "It's not all your fault. We could have visited you, I guess."

"It's not your mother's fault," he said.

I didn't think so either. "She works long hours," I said. Because I wanted him to feel good, I added, "Probably she did need you, now and again." I realized then that might be the wrong thing to say. "Not that you should feel bad. Aunt Ginny and Suzie are usually around. There's Mrs. Buttermark too."

Granddad was kind of standing in the water, not even treading, staring into space across the pool. Then I realized, he *was* standing in the water. I wasn't in what could technically be called the deep end anymore.

But I didn't like that staring.

I mean, there's times when my mom is translating and she stares off, trying out different words in her head. Then there's times when she thinks about my dad who died seven years ago, or her parents who died before that, and she stares in a different way. Granddad was staring in that different way.

I pulled myself past him for shallower water.

"I don't like the way the water feels heavy on my chest," I told him. "It makes me nervous."

He stopped staring. "It makes you stronger, fighting that," he said, following me. "Once you can swim, it doesn't scare you so much. You always notice it, though. That's a good thing. It keeps you careful."

"Because even people who can swim can drown?"

"It happens."

"Well, I'm going to pull myself along to the deep end again," I said, "unless you're ready to go." I was tired of hanging around in the same spot.

"Try this," Granddad said. "Take a deep breath and hold it here where you can touch bottom. Do a deep knee bend, and when you come up, come up fast. We used to call them cannonballs. That fast."

I didn't really want to do it, but he was right, I could stand up now too. I didn't really have a good excuse to say no.

I didn't like it when the water closed over my head. The weight on my chest was worse. I didn't like water in my eyes normally. But I needed to open them now. It was weird how that was true.

Once I was squatting on the bottom I pushed off hard.

It was like pressing up against a heavy blanket. More work than I expected. And then I broke through the surface with a rush of water skimming off me and the weight was gone. I think I yelled or laughed, I'm not sure. My feet left the bottom and it felt fine to be practically flying out of the water.

It only lasted a second but it was good. Great.

I shook my head and water flew. My eyelashes were wet and stuck to my cheeks for a second, but it didn't bother me this time. "Cannonball!"

Granddad nodded, looking like he was having fun too. "That's what your dad called them."

We had a moment there. I could feel the space where my dad would've been once. Usually I felt like Mom was holding that space for me. Now Granddad was holding it and it was as if I had stepped in, something I'd never been able to do before.

"I'll do a few more laps," Granddad said, and the moment was over. "The warm water feels good. Then we'll head over to the hospital."

I did have a little feeling like a sigh. Part of me was still ready to leave. But another part wouldn't mind doing a few more cannonballs. "Okay," I said. "Visiting hours won't start till later."

"Visiting hours?" He looked like he'd never heard of them. "We're going to sneak some sandwiches in to your mom long before that. Hospital food is the worst. They can throw us out in the snow if they want, but we're feeding her first."

I'd heard about hospital food from Aunt Ginny. Even worse than the school cafeteria.

Granddad swam a few more laps. I did cannon-balls. And then I pulled myself all the way to where the diving board is. The weight on my chest didn't bother me that much anymore. The warm water felt good to my tailbone.

This wasn't so much bravery as it was that I'd started to like Granddad. He talked like a guy who was used to getting thrown out of places. Thrown out, and not bothered by it in the least.

CHAPTER
ELEVEN

They didn't throw us out. It was almost a disappointment, how easy it was to see Mom and hang around in her room. We found somebody to give her TV service for when we weren't there.

Mom could only sit up halfway, because of her leg. She wore the flannel nightgown Mrs. Buttermark had brought her. She had some leggings too, since she couldn't cover up very well with one leg hanging in the air.

"That was my biggest problem during the night," Mom said. "The room got a little cold and I was under this tented blanket and I couldn't warm up the air space around me."

Granddad said, "Maybe we can bring in an electric heater for tonight."

"They brought me one," Mom said. "They took it

away a few minutes before you and Jake showed up. I'm fine, Ned. Did I thank you yesterday for coming here so quickly? I can't remember."

He seemed embarrassed to be reminded.

I said, "You did."

Granddad said, "Tell us what you want for dinner. Italian food? Chinese?"

"Oh, anything. What have you guys been up to?"

"Swimming," I said, as if I did it every day.

"Cool," Mom said, as if I did it every day.

"We unpacked the groceries," I said. "I brought you the cookies. They're probably frozen, though."

"The groceries," Mom said. "That seems like years ago. What day is it?"

"Monday."

"Don't you have—oh, Jake, today's the Christmas party."

"This is where I'd rather be," I said.

"Well, it's where I'm happy to have you right now," Mom said. "I'm sorry you missed the party."

"No big deal. There'll be another one next year."

It wasn't long before we broke out the sandwiches. As it turns out, four pancakes don't go far when you go swimming first thing in the morning.

We talked and laughed a little between bites.

Granddad went out for a smoke, which gave me a chance to tell Mom about his scary dog.

"You didn't used to be scared of that dog," Mom said. "He was a little scared of you."

"Because I tried to pull his tail."

Mom laughed. "You remember that?"

"Granddad told me."

"We kept finding that dog in your crib. Or you eating out of his food dish."

"Yuck."

Granddad came in then and told a few stories of his own. He made it seem funny that he had to sit out on the fire escape to smoke a cigarette.

Mom looked at us both like we'd lost our minds.

"Smoking is hot work. I felt fine." Granddad said that, and then he sneezed.

"Oh, no. You've caught a cold," Mom said.

"One sneeze," Granddad said.

The nurse was going by and she looked in. She said, "It's my job to send away people with sneezes unless they're in a bed."

"One sneeze," Granddad said. "I don't catch colds."

The nurse eyed the sandwiches. "I can be bribed with food."

I got the peanut butter and banana sandwich and counted myself lucky. Mrs. Buttermark puts these strange lettuces on the ones with meat and cheese. Basil and arugula and stuff.

The nurse thought very highly of strange lettuce. "Mozzarella with basil, how does that sound?" Granddad said.

"Heavenly."

Granddad sneezed again, and she said, "Sounds like you do have a cold."

"Not me," Granddad said. "I never catch cold." He thumped himself on the chest a couple of times. "Hardy."

"Lives in the South," Mom said, folding her sandwich bag neatly. Folding something neatly is what she does when she's getting tired or bored or nervous, whether it's a napkin or the paper from a straw. I figured she was tired.

"Buy yourself a scarf to wear while you're here," the nurse said to Granddad. She looked over her shoulder as she was leaving with her sandwich. "Better go buy it now."

I said, "We'll come back later."

"What?" Mom said. "You don't have to go."

"We have errands to run," Granddad said. "Give us a list of what to bring you. Do you want a paper-back book?"

"More magazines," Mom said. "Anything with pictures. They relax me." I had a feeling hospitals didn't have nearly as many rules as schools, but it still didn't feel like a fun place to be.

We'd stepped out of her room when Mom called me back. She said, "Are you okay?"

I shrugged. "I'm having a good time, kind of. Even the swimming and the scary dog are fine."

"He's a lot like your dad, I think you should know."

I didn't know what to say to that. Except "He smokes Camels. Isn't that weird?"

"Not at all."

Mom did look tired. "We'll see you later," I said, and reached up and ruffled her hair the way she usually did to me. I think we both felt better.

Granddad found a store with nothing *but* magazines. Except for gum and candy bars and cigarettes, that sort of thing. He bought a ton of magazines, mostly about travel.

Also flowers, because I told him Mom and Aunt Ginny like to garden in pots on the rooftop. We got

Cat Fancy and a few science magazines. Strange science, the kind Suzie likes.

He also bought a package of tissues because he sneezed a few more times. I reminded him about the scarf. He sneezed again while we were looking for a store that sold them.

"You didn't dry your hair," I said. "After the swim."

He gave me a raised-eyebrow look. I thought he probably figured he didn't have all that much hair. "Aunt Ginny has hair nearly as short as yours," I said. "She says she has to dry her head with a hair dryer before she goes out."

He said, "I've never used a hair dryer."

"Probably it's warmer in North Carolina. You aren't used to how cold it is here."

He sneezed again. "Good point."

CHAPTER TWELVE

Mom was asleep during visiting hours. We sneaked in and left the magazines for her. Granddad wrote a note like the one I'd left him, telling her we'd bring food later. Before she was forced to eat hospital food.

I wrote a note saying we'd left the cookies for her in case of a hunger emergency.

Then we went to the grocery store for things we'd had to throw away. Granddad bought those bags of lettuce that Mrs. Buttermark used in her sandwiches.

Then he spotted the loose candy in jars. "Jellies," he said. "I haven't had these in years." He took them out of the jar with his fingers and handed one to me before he ate one.

"You're supposed to use the scoop to put them in a plastic bag," I said.

"That's a plan." He was quick about it, as if he'd

been ordered to buy candies. I ate the one he'd given me and it was really good. Chocolate on the outside, raspberry jellied candy on the inside. He was loading up, and saying, "Let's get the orange-flavored ones too."

I had to tell him we couldn't eat any more until we paid for them. It was sort of funny; he looked awfully disappointed. We went on with what he called "more important" shopping.

He knew practically everything there was to know about avocados. When he was in the marines, he'd lived someplace in Central America where they were grown. He kept squeezing the avocados and putting them down. He didn't take any.

He moved on to mangos. He sniffed these before squeezing them and turning them all down. I'd seen Aunt Ginny say, I'll run into the store for an avocado, and do it.

Granddad was not that kind of person. If he was some guy in a movie, Aunt Ginny and Mom would've laughed till tears ran down their cheeks. Except Mom's the same way about tomatoes. She likes to grow her own. She starts them on the shelf under the aquarium. They finish growing up on the roof.

I stood on the other side of the cart while he was

sniffing and squeezing, and I smelled the parsley and cilantro he put into it. These are the only things, after the tomatoes, that Mom bothers to pinch or smell. It's hard to tell them apart.

I looked around, wondering if I looked funny too. I saw that old lady from the parking lot farther down the aisle. She'd gone past the fruit and veggies to the section where there were flowers in pots.

She seemed to be admiring some houseplants with big pink and green leaves. She'd pick one up and then put it back, like Granddad with the avocados. She picked up the ones with a lot of pink in them, so I figured she liked those best.

While she looked the plants over, I thought of going up to her and saying, *Thanks, you were a big help the other day. My mom is going to be good as new.*

I wondered if the old lady would even know it was me. If there'd be this embarrassing moment where I'd have to explain it was my mother who fell on the ice. Maybe I'd have to say she had to be operated on and now I was living with my granddad, or he was living with me. To tell you the truth, I thought I might cry.

Stupid, I know.

She turned away from the plants and saw me. She waved and started our way. I was glad I didn't have to explain who I was, but now I had to explain who she was.

"Granddad."

"Yep?" He'd started talking more like a regular person and less like those military guys you see in movies. He was choosing bananas with freckles.

I pointed. "That lady coming over here yelled for help when Mom fell." He didn't wait for me to say I wanted to thank her. He went to meet her and introduced himself. Us.

She put out her hand. "Lillian Martin. Call me Lillian. If you call me Martin, someone will expect me to have a mustache."

Granddad looked surprised to hear her make a joke right off the bat. Me too. It made me grin to see him look like he wasn't quite sure what to say. He pulled himself together real well, though.

"We're very grateful that you have a good pair of lungs on you," Granddad said. "Wouldn't have expected it, looking at you. Size of a kitten."

Lillian got all pink and fluttery. I figured they liked each other. Not like Lillian might be coming over to dinner or something. But it helps to like somebody you run into a lot.

Granddad thanked her so that I didn't have to say

a thing, really. I did say, "You were great." And then, just what I was afraid of, I got that feeling I might cry again.

I shut up and let Granddad talk to her.

I wasn't listening. I had to wonder how long I was going to go around feeling like a big crybaby. I doubted I was going to impress Granddad much if this happened too often.

When Lillian Martin left us to finish her shopping, Granddad went over to those plants. He grabbed up three of them and gave me the money to pay for them. They were mostly light and dark green.

I said, "Are these for her?" because it seemed to me he waited for her to go around a corner.

"They are." He seemed a little embarrassed himself.

"She liked the ones with more pink."

So we switched them. I gave Granddad my shopping list and I went off to wait for Mrs. Martin at the door. I helped her out to her car.

"It's still icy out here," I said when she told me what a little gentleman I was. She sounded a lot like Mrs. Buttermark. I sounded a lot like Granddad, I thought, except my voice wasn't as deep.

I had the plants in brown paper sacks so she

couldn't see them yet. I figured they might not get as cold as they would in a thin plastic bag. Once we got outside, I decided fur coats wouldn't have kept them warm.

Luckily, she was parked close to the store. "I'm more careful since your mother's accident," she said to me.

I put everything on the seat. She noticed the brown paper sacks then and said, "Oh, those aren't mine."

"Granddad and I wanted to give you something for a thank-you."

She peeked into one of the sacks and said "Oh," like a little meow. "You're a special boy."

"It was Granddad's idea," I said.

She kissed me on top of my head anyhow, the way I've made Mom stop doing. It was nice, though.

CHAPTER THIRTEEN

We went home to walk the dog. Max.

He acted like a different dog entirely.

He ran into the hall and wiggled all over the place with happiness when he saw Granddad. He didn't bark at me or show his teeth. He didn't ignore me either. He sniffed at my pant leg and gave a little sneeze.

I figured Mrs. Buttermark must have been thinking nice things about dogs and reflecting them onto Max all day long.

"We did some shopping," Granddad said. He handed Mrs. Buttermark some bags of lettuce. Plants too, the same ones with pink leaves.

She looked surprised, and laughed. "Thank you, both," she said. "I love these. I always mean to get a couple. Then, by the time I fill up my cart . . ." She shrugged.

I was glad Granddad had brought her some plants. I didn't know how much she liked them until I saw her in the flower store, buying for Mom and even for the waiting room.

We put the lettuce and apples and bananas in our fridge. By then Max was standing on his hind feet, dancing around us. He was sort of cute.

If you like dogs.

We took him out. I noticed he was pretty cheerful about walks. His tail wagged faster or slower, depending on what he thought was most interesting.

Granddad had me hold Max's leash for a minute while we walked him. He said he had to buy a paper. He said he couldn't get along without a crossword puzzle. We walked a block or two with me holding the leash, passing one place where Granddad could've gone in for what he wanted.

Plus, he'd already done that when we got magazines for Mom. He could also have gotten cigarettes at the grocery store. I think Granddad mostly wanted Max to know he was supposed to trust me.

Granddad finally picked a store where he wanted to shop. A ladies' shop, full of bath stuff and hair combs and change purses and little blankets to put over your legs when you're watching TV. I'd been in there a lot of times with Aunt Ginny. Max watched Granddad go, his stubby tail wilting like a plant that needed water.

Max looked at me the minute Granddad went through the door. "Good boy," I said.

He looked away.

I sort of knew how he felt. That time we were puppies together was a long time ago. We didn't really remember each other the way Granddad hoped. Max wasn't crazy about me. Some part of him knew I wasn't crazy about him either. That probably I was saying something nice to cover it up. So far, he was right.

I was trying, though.

I thought about how he wriggled around Granddad's ankles, so happy. How he danced around in our kitchen.

I'd gone to a science expo with Mom and Suzie the year before. We looked at weird science. Water running uphill, then down, then up again, through an up-and-downhill maze, like a rat, because the water wanted to find its way back to where it came from.

I saw a car that ran on corn oil.

I saw proof that everything, people, animals, paramecium—vegetables, even—have light shining from them all the time. It was possible to take pictures of that light. It even shone from a maple leaf with a corner torn away—it shone as if the leaf was still all there.

At the time, I thought it was more exciting that I went to New York City and rode in a subway. Stayed in a hotel and ordered room service.

I thought about the fact that everything has a little light in them. Aunt Ginny's idea of reflecting made sense to me.

Max looked at me again, like maybe he was getting used to me. I imagined I could see that light in him and reflected it with a big smile.

He sat down and then he stood up again because the ground was cold. I remembered he'd been sick lately and he was old, even if he didn't look it to me.

Granddad was taking his time coming out, so I walked Max along the street until we'd passed two stores and then I turned around and walked him the other way. This was so Granddad would see us when he came outside.

Max looked nervous about the whole thing. Me walking him, and no doubt he wasn't quite used to being reflected at so much. Probably the last few days hadn't been easy for him either, hanging around by himself in the car and then in the apartment.

I made up my mind to sleep in my bed that night.

Partly, I had the feeling Max understood now, I belonged there. And partly, he probably got it that Granddad wanted us to get along. If there was one thing I knew about Max, it was how much he tried to please Granddad.

When Granddad came out, I still had to hold Max's leash, because Granddad had too many bags to carry and walk his dog at the same time.

Mrs. Buttermark was dressed to go out when we got upstairs. She was coming to the hospital with us, although we weren't going until we'd eaten. Granddad said sometimes he had to eat as soon as he got hungry or he felt peckish, whatever that is.

"Are you catching a cold?" Mrs. Buttermark asked Granddad. "You sound a little stuffed up."

"No, no," he said. "I have a turtleneck in my suitcase."

"Well, it won't do you a bit of good if you leave it there," Mrs. Buttermark told him. What really amazed me, Granddad grinned. "I made fresh sandwiches," she said, sort of ignoring this miracle. "All we have to do is unzip them."

"I could wait until we get to the hospital," Granddad said.

"No, no," Mrs. Buttermark said, heading for her

kitchen. "We can't have anyone feeling peckish. Besides, these sandwiches are best if they're eaten right away." Mrs. Buttermark turned to me and said, "Would you like a cream cheese and olive sandwich?"

"No, thanks," I said. "Peanut butter and jelly will be good."

We sat down at her usual window spot, with an extra chair pulled up to the table. "Do you by any chance play chess?" Mrs. Buttermark asked Granddad.

"I used to, but it's been years," Granddad said.

"Your grandson is a strong player," Mrs. Buttermark said.

"You don't say."

"Yeah, play with me," I said, "because you'll never win if you play against Mrs. Buttermark. That's what she isn't telling you."

They went on talking about the game.

I noticed Mrs. Buttermark had spruced up her place since we left that morning. Dusted, okay, but also washed or polished. Things looked like she'd spent the whole day taking care of them.

The thing Mrs. Buttermark doesn't do much of is cooking and housework. Even her Christmas tree lights had already been turned on. I'm sorry to say she saw me noticing.

"Having fresh company has brought me up to speed," Mrs. Buttermark said. "I'm afraid things had gotten a little drab around here."

"Don't do anything on my account," Granddad said. "Everything they say about men living alone is true. I have a young mother living next door who does my housework. It helps us both out."

Mrs. Buttermark said, "About housework. I did the math. It doesn't pay."

I remembered her telling Mom it takes her four minutes to clean her kitchen sink and wipe it dry. Four minutes at least twice a day to keep it looking good. So 375 days a year, that's 3,000 minutes, or 50 hours, or more than two days of that year. For weeks after, Mom was doing the math on all kinds of stuff we do around the house.

"I made up my mind to wash my dishes once a day and count that as cleaning my sink. I do a real sink cleaning once a week," Mrs. Buttermark was telling Granddad. "By the end of one year, I've washed my sink for less than three and a half hours instead of more than two days, leaving me forty-eight hours, or two days, to do something more interesting."

"I like the way you think," Granddad said.

"If I live with a few dust bunnies, so be it," Mrs.

Buttermark said. "I heard on TV every old person should have a pet. It helps us live longer."

"You're hardly an old person," Granddad said.

Both of them blushed. I pretended not to notice. They made me blush too, I think. I got embarrassed in some weird way.

"How about some tea?" Mrs. Buttermark said. "I hear it's good for a cold."

"Never catch the things, myself," Granddad said.

"Well, then, let's get over to the hospital," Mrs. Buttermark said. "Was your sandwich okay?"

"Best I ever had," Granddad said. He'd eaten two.

Here's what I know about Mrs. Buttermark: cream cheese and chopped green olive sandwiches are what she makes when she wants to impress somebody.

Granddad did look impressed.

CHAPTER FOURTEEN

"It's time we took a meal over to your mother," Granddad said as we were putting on our coats. "Serious food."

"Egg rolls and orange chicken," I said. It took me about one second to figure out this wasn't Granddad's idea of serious food. "It puts Mom in a good mood."

"That's it, then," Mrs. Buttermark said. "That's as serious as we get around here."

"I'll put Max in Liz's apartment," Granddad said. "He'll be fine until we get back."

Mom had a food tray on the bed table when we got there. Under a lid, there was some kind of chicken and rice dish sinking into a thick gravy and gray peas. Yuck.

"Eat this," Granddad said, eyeing the plate as he handed over the orange chicken. "We'll use the container to make a doggie bag for Max. He'll think he's died and gone to heaven."

"I know how he's going to feel," Mom said, opening the container and taking a deep breath.

While Mom ate, Mrs. Buttermark told us what good company Max turned out to be. I told them about Granddad buying the old lady some plants. How happy she was to have them.

Granddad changed the subject by saying, "Since you won't be home for Christmas, Liz, I think we ought to talk about how to bring it to you."

"Christmas Eve," Mom said. "It's tomorrow? I've completely lost track of time."

Me too.

"Do you open gifts in the morning or the night before?" he asked, like he was Captain Christmas. It was nice.

"A little of each," Mom said.

"For the last few years, I've been joining them," Mrs. Buttermark said.

"Last year we had a pajama party with Ginny and Suzie," Mom said. "We haven't told them about this yet. Oh, I haven't thought about anything outside this room, have I?"

"Please," Granddad said. "Donna and I hoped you wouldn't have to."

"We can have a party here tomorrow night, as late as the hospital will allow us to stay," Mrs. Buttermark said. "Then we'll be back first thing Christmas morning. I'm sure we won't be the only family with this plan."

I don't know if Mom or Mrs. Buttermark or Granddad noticed she called us a family. They started planning how to do things.

But I noticed. I liked it. That's all.

The next morning, Granddad woke up sick.

I said, "I don't think you should go out."

"I hab to," he said, looking over at his dog. Whenever anybody talked about going out, that dog came to attention. I'm serious. It sat like a little soldier.

I said, "He'd probably salute if he knew how."

Granddad gave me an odd look and then grinned. "Max," he said, and saluted the dog.

He lifted one paw and brushed at his ear.

"Wow," I said. Okay, he brushed a couple of times. It wasn't a real salute. It was impressive, though. I tried to reflect how impressive I thought that was. I sent Max the best beam-me-up-Scotty look I could muster.

"I'm taking him out," I said. "I'll call Mr. G. He has a pretty old dog, so Max will be comfortable. I can walk with him after dark tonight."

Granddad looked like he was about to say no. He felt his forehead for fever and said yes. That is, he said, "I think you'b god a good idea there."

Aunt Ginny is right. Ten is a turning point, maturity-wise.

I said, "First I'm going to let Mrs. Buttermark know your cold is worse."

"Ohhh," he said, like this was his worst nightmare.

"Don't worry," I said. "She has a cure. Three days from now you won't know you had a sniffle."

I sounded the alarm.

"Oh, dear," Mrs. Buttermark said. "I'll put on the tea."

"I'll come help squeeze the lemons and oranges after I walk the dog."

"Tell Ned not to eat a thing."

"I remember," I said. "If you feed a cold, you have to starve a fever."

I went to our apartment and put the leash on the dog. Actually, I held the leash out and waited to see how he'd react to this idea. We hadn't consulted him.

He came to me. He didn't look thrilled about it. He looked at me like I was wearing a name tag that read STAN. Not that he could read it even if I was. I was the substitute for what he really wanted and he knew he had to deal with it.

"Don' led him loose in the dog run," Granddad said. "He isn't strong jus' now. If some bid dod picks on him, he can' defend himself."

Max looked perfectly capable of defending himself. It was fine with me if he didn't get to run around with the other dogs. I didn't care to bump into those dogs myself.

Max's tail went up the minute we hit the lobby. Tail up means: getting down to business. Outside, he went from tree to tree, peeing in little spurts. Everybody knows this is a message another dog will come along and read. Sniffing is reading. That's how dogs operate.

He didn't take any notice of other dogs writing

the same message, though. He was trotting along pretty fast between short stops. I figured he was just interested in getting to the apartment, where it was warm.

That was what I wanted too. We had something in common besides being puppies together—cold feet. I sent a sunny smile straight at him, even though he wasn't looking at me. I hoped reflecting worked like that.

The other thing I noticed, Max's tail wagged the whole time we were out there. I felt good about that. I really did. It probably didn't have a thing to do with me, though. He wagged his tail a lot of the time.

As soon as I opened the door, Max raced in to let Granddad know he was back. I heard him jump on the bed and Granddad telling him about his wet feet. He sounded like wet feet were something to be proud of, and I realized Mrs. Buttermark was right—Granddad was crazy about that dog.

Aunt Ginny called in while I was taking off my shoes and leaving them by the door. She'd gotten home and heard our message. She started the conversation with, "How's your mom?"

"She got operated on," I said. "Now she wants magazines and Mrs. Buttermark's sandwiches."

"Everybody wants Donna's sandwiches," Aunt Ginny said. "If ever I don't want one of Donna's sandwiches, you'll know I've died."

I lowered my voice. "Granddad's here with me."

She whispered, "Sitting next to you?"

I whispered back, "On the sofa bed in Mom's office. He caught a cold."

"Is he what you expected?" she said, still talking low.

"I didn't know what to expect," I said, using the low voice.

"Come on," she said. "You know what I mean."

"He's not somebody I'd walk up to at the school book fair and say, hey, you could be my granddad," I said. "He looks like somebody I might see somewhere and think he might be cool."

"Good. That's good."

"We went swimming, that's how he caught cold."

"The plot thickens."

"Huh?"

"*You* went swimming? There's a lot to this story you haven't told me yet."

"Listen, will you visit Mom this morning? We're going to be busy here, making tea and stuff. We were going to sit around the hospital with Mom. I don't think Granddad can go now."

"Let me talk to him. Don't get him out of bed. I'll hold on while you go give him the office phone."

I hung around to see if I needed to explain anything. Granddad did fine, giving Aunt Ginny the details on Mom. He filled her in on our plans.

Suzie checked in later in the day, when she got home. Mrs. Buttermark picked up the phone. They talked in whispers. At least Mrs. Buttermark did.

And then I talked to her. "Earmuffs," Suzie said instead of hello. "What do you think of them?"

"For who?"

"Anybody. Are they something only dorks wear or are they an acceptable item of clothing?"

"They're pretty dorky," I said. I couldn't remember seeing anybody cool wearing them.

"What if you were skiing? Would you wear them then?"

"Suzie, are you going skiing?" I hoped she wasn't going to miss Christmas.

"Would your granddad like them?"

"Oh." I lowered my voice. "I think a warm hat would be good. No pom-poms or anything. Black, I guess."

"Any other ideas? Something from you."

I usually signed my name to the cigars Mom bought. I tried hard to think of what kids send their grandparents. I saw Granddad's shoes by the door and hurried over there. "Slippers," I whispered. I looked inside his shoe and found a number stamped on the side. "Size eleven and a half."

CHAPTER FIFTEEN

Here's how we worked Christmas out. Aunt Ginny and Suzie and I would spend Christmas Eve at the hospital with Mom. Granddad's cigars had already been shipped to North Carolina, so Aunt Ginny took me with her to buy some more.

"What else?" she said to me. "We want him to feel Christmasy."

So I said, "Let's go to the grocery store." I bought pancake mix and orange marmalade in a little white crock because he'd said to Mrs. Buttermark that he liked it, and another pound of chocolate-covered jellies. The ones we got earlier were already gone.

We bought Meaty Bones and pigs' ears for Max.

We stopped into a bookstore and got crossword puzzles, and Aunt Ginny got him a dark red scarf in the same mall. We wrapped those presents for Granddad.

Then I called Mr. G.

It was dicey getting Max together with Mr. G's dog. Max had that *little dog, big attitude* attitude. Mr. G's dog was big enough to eat him if Max ticked him off. I hoped Max noticed.

At first he kept his tail straight up in the air, and a little collar of fur rose up around his neck. Mr. G's dog, named Moose, ignored him.

Mr. G had about a hundred falling-on-the-ice stories to tell me. Talking in the cold didn't seem to bother his teeth at all. "Uh-huh," or a shake of the head, that's all I had to say to keep Mr. G happy.

By the time we got home, Max and Moose acted like they were old buddies, laughing in each other's faces. I couldn't get over it. Dogs are weird.

Suzie had also done some shopping for Granddad—including a chess set, a gift from Mrs. Buttermark. That's what the whispers were about.

Mrs. Buttermark spent the evening with Granddad and Max. They listened to Christmas carols and worked on a jigsaw puzzle of sunny Italy. They'd both been there and were telling each other what they'd done.

Aunt Ginny and Suzie and I sat with Mom. We

opened small presents that were easy to carry. Mom and I gave Suzie a remote-controlled spider we'd bought months before. We could hardly wait to give it to her. It was even hairy.

Suzie didn't disappoint us with her reaction. She screamed. "We could name it," I said, and got a laugh.

We gave Aunt Ginny a T-shirt with a picture of Mount Kilimanjaro on it. She plans to climb it one day. And Aunt Ginny gave Mom a set of markers, thirty-six colors, to make her cast look good. I gave Mom the sweater Aunt Ginny helped me pick out, because the hospital could get a little cold.

Suzie gave me a remote-controlled spider too. I screamed like Suzie, on purpose.

We took them for a walk down the hospital corridor and got bigger laughs. I named mine Boris. Suzie called hers Lucy.

That night, after I went to bed, Mrs. Buttermark stayed to watch a movie with Granddad, an old Christmas movie they both liked. They talked through most of it. It's hard getting to sleep on Christmas Eve, so it was kind of nice to listen to them telling stories about themselves.

I learned Mrs. Buttermark had been a rocket. That

made me sit up. She and Granddad talked about it a little and I realized it was some kind of dancer.

And then Mrs. Buttermark asked what life was like in North Carolina. "I'm a little too set in my ways there," Granddad said. "Like those fish in that tank there. Easy ways. It could be a lot more interesting and I'd be happier. It's been interesting here."

Which struck me as a lot for Granddad to say all at once. He didn't sound like the words were being yanked all the way from his toes, the way he sometimes did with me. I figured Mrs. Buttermark had been reflecting at him. She brought out the best in him.

Mrs. Buttermark and Suzie rang the doorbell first thing Christmas morning. I'd been lying in bed for a while. Half asleep, just not ready to get up—I could smell custard baking, a Christmas-morning specialty that I figured Aunt Ginny came in early to make. It seemed weird that everything was so different this year. Not terrible or anything. Mom would be home in another day or two.

I heard the apartment door open, and Suzie was talking about learning how to make Mrs. Buttermark's French toast. Max came skittering along the hall and stopped at my room like he had a message to deliver.

I sat up in bed and stared at him. We were getting pretty friendly, but I wasn't asking him up onto my bed or anything. I got dressed in the bathroom. I wasn't missing anything. On Christmas morning, it's breakfast first, then gifts.

When I came out, I could hear everybody in the living room, and forks hitting plates. I was getting pretty hungry myself. The first thing I spotted, in front of the tree, was a red mountain bike.

"Wow!"

I felt like Aunt Ginny at the top of Kilimanjaro. Like Suzie when she gets her first sight of something amazing. Like Mom when she does her little dance of finding just the right words for a translation.

I felt like I'd just done a cannonball.

I looked at Granddad.

"Not from me," he said, waving his fork.

"Your mom didn't want you to have to wait till she came home," Suzie said. "Besides, you can't ride anywhere but down the hall and around the lobby until the snow melts."

"Mom got me a bike?"

"Let's make up a song called 'After All These Years,' " Aunt Ginny said, laughing a little.

"Your mom got you a bike and I got you a helmet,"

Mrs. Buttermark said, pointing to a big silver package with her fork. "Now come and eat your breakfast. Max has been eyeing your plate."

I ate fast. I could hardly wait to get to the hospital to see Mom. We didn't even bother to open any gifts.

Suzie and Aunt Ginny had planned to help Granddad make a Christmas turkey with all the trimmings. The turkey had already been put in the oven when Aunt Ginny showed up. Granddad knew how.

So Suzie and Aunt Ginny were in charge of the trimmings. And Granddad was going to watch a game on television unless they needed some help.

Mrs. Buttermark and I went over to the hospital.

Mom was sitting in a chair with her leg propped up. There was Christmas music playing on the television.

"Mom, the bike is a beauty."

"I figured you couldn't go on riding Joey's bike your whole life," she said with a grin. "Or how are the two of you ever going to make any time?"

"You knew?"

"I saw you one day, and Joey was jogging along behind. He looked hot and tired and like a really good friend. I figured you ought to have your own bike, for both your sakes."

"Where'd you hide it?"

"At my place, of course," Mrs. Buttermark said. "When you came to stay, I had to fit it in to my bedroom closet. That was a challenge."

She brought out a refrigerator dish for Mom. Inside it was a glass dish with a baked custard.

I unpacked the presents we carried over to open with Mom. She said, "This is the laziest Christmas I've had in a long time."

In the afternoon, Aunt Ginny and Suzie traded places with us. They brought some Christmas dinner to eat with Mom. Mrs. Buttermark drove me home to eat with Granddad and Max.

I opened two gifts from Granddad. One was a framed picture of Mom and my dad, and I was sitting on Dad's lap for the photo. I looked a little surprised by the whole thing, but Mom looked proud and Dad looked happy to be there. I'd never seen this picture before.

The other present was a set of small warrior figures on horseback.

Some of the men wore colorful scarflike outfits,

and the others were dressed in blue and white, in white shirts with flowing sleeves. Even the horses were dressed up with scarves and feathers, the wind lifting the scarves and sleeves so men and horses looked like they were in motion. I'd never seen anything quite like them. They gave me a little chill.

They were the Greeks and Persians, Granddad told me. "Your dad was kind of a history buff. These belonged to him once."

Goose bumps, that's what they gave me.

That's what Granddad said his gifts did for him. Mrs. Buttermark had accidentally given him a book he'd been wanting, a book of famous ships.

That evening, Granddad and Mrs. Buttermark went over to the hospital. Suzie and Aunt Ginny opened the rest of their gifts with me. It felt like Christmas was going on and on and on, which was fine by me.

Mom was home for New Year's Eve and we did the holiday sleepover. She could get around in this narrow little wheelchair that Aunt Ginny had rented.

Granddad's cold was gone and Mrs. Buttermark was over at our place more than she was at home in her apartment. That was fine with everybody. Especially Granddad.

Joey Ziglar was back from Florida and he came over too, with his dog. He and Aunt Ginny could hardly shut up about Arizona. Which was very cool. Joey has a major crush on Aunt Ginny.

Max hardly knew what to do with himself, visiting with a dog the same size. And Joey's dog woke up to acting like a dog that had more on his mind than a leash, a food dish, and a nap.

They kept chasing each other all around the apartment, the sound of dog toenails up and down the hallway. Now and then one of them would body slam the other. They would pant hard in that laughing way, but they ran on without stopping.

There was a new jigsaw puzzle on the coffee table, half done. The chess table was out because Mom and Granddad had been playing the same game for two days.

He had another game going with Mrs. Buttermark. And her old set with the salt shaker was under the tree in case anybody else felt like playing.

Around eight o'clock, Mom and Aunt Ginny put on a movie and Joey and I got into our sleeping bags to watch with them.

Joey fell asleep halfway through the second one. Luckily, he was already in his sleeping bag. His dog was in there too. When we got to the Kleenex part of the movie, I went in and flopped on my bed for a while.

Mrs. Buttermark would sleep there tonight. I had a sleeping bag on the living room floor too. Max followed me in and hopped up on the bed with me. He flipped onto his back for a belly rub. I didn't even have to think about it. As bristly as most of his body is, the belly hair is soft, like the feathers on ducklings.

I thought, that's something to reflect back at him. While I was doing that, something weird happened. I saw him really sharp around the edges. I was going to have to tell Aunt Ginny about that.

Granddad came and sat on the edge of my bed. "Tearjerkers not your style?"

I shrugged. "They're okay."

"You haven't caught my cold?"

"Never catch cold," I said, making my voice deep. I pounded on my chest. "Hardy."

He jounced on the edge of my bed, jiggling me around. Max barked and jumped off the bed.

Granddad said, "Hey, do you remember this?" He started to sort of stand halfway up and sit down hard on the bed over and over, jiggling me a little. A lot.

Granddad bounced so hard I lifted off the mattress. Not as high as I used to, but that didn't matter. The jiggling made me feel like I was laughing. Maybe I was laughing. Max barked a few more times.

Mostly, it surprised me. Partly because Granddad was acting kind of silly, and I liked that. Also because I saw my memories weren't really pointless after all. I was seeing Granddad really sharp around the edges.

Granddad kept up the bouncing and pretty soon I was laughing like a maniac.

"I remember!" I shouted.

ACKNOWLEDGMENTS

For those of you who wonder,
and I know there are a lot of you—
teachers, librarians,
and often the young readers—
I'd like to point out the supportive cast of
characters at Random House who made this
book the beautiful object that it is.

* * *

Designer: Heather Palisi
Art director: Ellice Lee
Copy editor: Alison Kolani
Production manager: Dan Myers
Managing editor: Maren Greif
Illustrator: Antonio Javier Caparo

* * *

* * *

Last, not least, my editor, Shana Corey,
who always makes our shared work
the best it can be.
Thank you from the bottom of my heart!

ABOUT THE AUTHOR

Audrey Couloumbis's first book for children, *Getting Near to Baby,* won the Newbery Honor in 2000. Audrey is also the author of several other highly acclaimed books for young readers, including *The Misadventures of Maude March* (which was named a Book Sense 76 Pick and a New York Public Library 100 Titles for Reading and Sharing Selection, and won a National Parenting Publications Gold Award) and *Love Me Tender* (a Book Sense Children's Summer Pick), and coauthor of *War Games* (a *Horn Book* Fanfare Best Book of the Year and a Junior Library Guild Selection). Audrey lives in upstate New York and Florida with her dog, Phoebe, and Phoebe's two pet parakeets, Tweedle Dee and Tweedle Dum.